The Harvest

by Samuel D. Hunter

SAMUELFRENCH.COM   SAMUELFRENCH.CO.UK

FOR PRODUCTION ENQUIRIES

UNITED STATES AND CANADA
Info@SamuelFrench.com
1-866-598-8449

UNITED KINGDOM AND EUROPE
Plays@SamuelFrench.co.uk
020-7255-4302

Each title is subject to availability from Samuel French, depending upon country of performance. Please be aware that *THE HARVEST* may not be licensed by Samuel French in your territory. Professional and amateur producers should contact the nearest Samuel French office or licensing partner to verify availability.

MUSIC USE NOTE

Licensees are solely responsible for obtaining formal written permission from copyright owners to use copyrighted music in the performance of this play and are strongly cautioned to do so. If no such permission is obtained by the licensee, then the licensee must use only original music that the licensee owns and controls. Licensees are solely responsible and liable for all music clearances and shall indemnify the copyright owners of the play(s) and their licensing agent, Samuel French, against any costs, expenses, losses and liabilities arising from the use of music by licensees. Please contact the appropriate music licensing authority in your territory for the rights to any incidental music.

IMPORTANT BILLING AND CREDIT REQUIREMENTS

If you have obtained performance rights to this title, please refer to your licensing agreement for important billing and credit requirements.

THE HARVEST was commissioned and first produced by LCT3 (Paige Evans, outgoing artistic director; Evan Cabnet, incoming artistic director) at the Claire Tow Theater at Lincoln Center on October 24, 2016. The production was directed by Davis McCallum, with set design by Dane Laffrey, costume design by Jessica Pabst, lighting design by Eric Southern, sound design by Leah Gelpe, and the music director was David Dabbon. The production stage manager was Marisa Levy, and the assistant stage manager was Brett Anders. The cast was as follows:

JOSH . . . . Peter Mark Kendall

TOM . . . . .Gideon Glick

MICHAELA . . . . Leah Karpel

ADA . . . . .Zoë Winters

DENISE . . . . .Madeleine Martin

MARCUS . . . . .Christopher Sears

CHUCK . . . . .Scott Jaeck

THE HARVEST was developed, in part, through a residency at Space on Ryder Farm (Emily Simoness, co-founder and executive director).

THE HARVEST was first workshopped and received a staged reading through a residency with the White Heron Theatre in Nantucket, Massachusetts (Lynne Bolton, artistic director; Michael Kopko, executive director) on July 1, 2015. The reading was directed by Gordon Edelstein.

CHARACTERS

JOSH – Early twenties, male
TOM – Early twenties, male
MICHAELA – Late twenties, female
ADA – Mid-twenties, female
DENISE – Early twenties, female
MARCUS – Early twenties, male
CHUCK – Fifties, male

SETTING

The moldy furnished basement of a small church in Idaho Falls, Idaho. The church itself has been built fairly recently and fairly cheaply. A set of stairs leads up to the main meeting room. There is a small kitchenette off to one side, and a bathroom offstage. Strewn haphazardly in the room are folding chairs, various children's toys, videos, Christian tracts, and Bibles. An aging, out-of-tune upright piano is against the wall on one side of the stage.

TIME

The present.

AUTHOR'S NOTES

Dialogue written in italics is emphatic, deliberate; dialogue in ALL CAPS is impulsive, explosive.

A "/" indicates an overlap in dialogue. Whenever a "/" appears, the following line of dialogue should begin.

Ellipses (…) indicate when a character is trailing off, dashes (–) indicate where a character is being cut off, either by another character or themselves.

Dialogue in [brackets] is implied, not spoken.

Arabic phrases have been roughly transliterated.

THREE DAYS TO DEPARTURE

Afternoon.

(JOSH, DENISE, MARCUS, and TOM are all in various positions in the room – sitting, lying down, or standing – all keeping their distance from one another. They all have their eyes closed.)

(ADA watches them for a moment. She then moves to the kitchen, takes a Starbucks cup off the counter, takes a drink. She looks at them one last time, then closes her eyes as well.)

(A long silence. Everyone is still.)

ADA. In Jesus' name we pray.

(Another long silence.)

(Finally:)

…keso ba, ba elli ba sho nee…

(Silence.)

MARCUS. Jesus pray, pray spirit Jesus / pray spirit Jesus God oh Jesus God…

ADA. Kelli kutu reish rohoosh arkad kallee dorra. Rei loochay…

(Silence.)

TOM. Kray besh tono ish lock bee nada, kana. / Lah bee nono yosh berran mana kay, mana kay, mana kay. Yo tono bee tada law tow be no fada.

7

MARCUS. Jesus God is Lord Lord / is Jesus God sho no la dada berra ko nana Jesus Lord ko nana bah lesh bee no… Jesus Lord God is Jesus God – …

JOSH. Rei me ko kelli kuss rei. / Kala ma seedee la fa besh fi la la oh shala bah. Bo sholo ka fono yo ishi na mama kalla.

ADA. Mino tarash. Wa ta shan. / Sheesh delee ma ta gash ta ma.

DENISE. Keso tatata elli. Keso tata nona tata keso tatata.

> *(Pause. JOSH opens his eyes, looks at TOM. TOM looks back at him briefly, then looks away and moves away from JOSH. JOSH closes his eyes again.)*

ADA. Tara fa minosh, / tara ya la foro pro al aka.

DENISE. Ka rash shaka baka –

> *(MARCUS looks at DENISE. He moves over to DENISE, his eyes half-closed.)*

ADA. / Tara ma fino la, ma fino en la fetera. Jesus Lord.

DENISE. Ka rash baka baka, rash baka –

> *(MARCUS puts a hand on DENISE's shoulder. She looks at MARCUS, they speak in hushed tones.)*

TOM. / Ko no fara ta bee, sha ta ra shaka yaraf bra yania shara ta bra mina fa tow. Ra kara faw la sheena fo to.

DENISE. What?

MARCUS. You're doing it again.

DENISE. No I'm not.

JOSH. / Fo no tada fa lash go na tero fa, shona la fina bee na flo no keena fa.

MARCUS. Honey you're doing it again.

> *(MARCUS smiles lovingly at DENISE.)*

ADA. Jesus Lord kana fee lo / bo no Jesus God.

DENISE. *Okay sorry just –.*

> *(DENISE moves away from him, closes her eyes. MARCUS closes his eyes as well.)*

TOM. Krani ma to fada la shee, fo no kana ta. / Fo no kana ta! Fo do la ko shonna fa kee jo polla fa da, hish ma fini ree tish bi lada, o no kana tee.

JOSH. Tro ray bo nada ha, / veni loo bo na keena toe nay. Bo la reshi ma keena foh gah la, foh gah la teeny po losh.

MARCUS. Jesus is Lord / ko nota ba lah, Jesus God in Heaven Lord koona besh li fadi tanna, Jesus God borah yan fashi bo nah, Jesus God borah yan ali man tee do nana fah –

DENISE. *(A bit more stilted than before.)* Koona bah. Koona –, / poh la sho do. En sheena bee no taka bah lah. Udi ma bresh keena fa wosh shoni fa do. Shoni fa – do.

ADA. Kani fah / lo beena ta losh, feeda ka poola go mani kay la. Mani fa doni ven tremi fa ishy lo jona. Jesus Lord God shona fa.

TOM. Shoni ma la yosh fenti mah, yosh fenti mah! *Yosh fenti ma, gona fee da!*

> *(**TOM** is overcome a bit, stands up, his face raised to God. **ADA** starts wandering around the room as she speaks.)*

JOSH. Shoni pah la! / Shoni esh mani kay, Jesus Lord God shona esh mani.

TOM. Kelli kan / tremi van kay, elli fa no shoni bo kala fa to –

MARCUS. / Alli kay tanda ma fesh Jesus Lord God tanda ray mah –

ADA. / Kali ma shay fan, telli mish ka no won do, kona to –

DENISE. Yo shosh tola la na keni, fo no shona –

> *(**DENISE** stretches out her arms and bumps **ADA**. **ADA** and **DENISE** immediately open their eyes, look at each other.)*

Crap sorry. Crap.

> *(**ADA** smiles at her icily, moving away. **JOSH** looks at **TOM**, **TOM** looks away, closes his eyes.)*

(Pause.)

ADA. ...mana la ta... Dona moshel keli ta / lana fa...

MARCUS. Fara to... Jesus God marana fa na, / lashni fo
toru tadik...

DENISE. Horu fada keeshtee, mini ya rama sorama...

(Pause.)

ADA. Kana sho la fadi kay. / Kona fa elli ba noda, fa noda
tra mani lee dono. Kani fa tee veni la bish shima kay, to
la fadi ma. Kesh shoko ola vey, hale ma sota man sana
ganta, ha so mola ka deko, al dolo chabi, asham rof
batain. Lama sohuda, sam prapa ne, yan teenchay no
baka fo la.

MARCUS. Jesus God fona to. Jesus God Heaven / Lord
Jesus bemi la fishee kay... Jesus is Lord, Jesus eso tora
dee pra dem, sora tee brata, may cheff ray skana pah ya
monote. Para toh say. Teek num bara ta, Jesus God is
Lord Jesus tala fara sho.

JOSH. Ho la mish fodi la, mish fodi la to ray loochay bi
shina krass va toor. / Ban se ton tante, ra tee so doray
lora nee, so kona mana hey so borota. Borota so lah sto
stana maya. Lora su to tare. Ma resh su roh kro, malata
fa no.

DENISE. Koli ma toni shandi polli fad. / Trey mi bani fo
trelli sta. Lambra tosh yanada pro fadi, yesu bambay,
falona fa shora ta dee. Tora fasha la koni ta, la koni ta
ba mi. Oh kando fa bra lo, fa tonti ma sho ba.

TOM. Kona bay mani tee la fodi. Alla kay tra bishnee for
nan boka fish tada. / Oh rah su pro pare, suto la tah
dee... Tee numra sha...

JOSH. Kelli ma teena fa bishee, / loka mo tish, fona ray see
krass vish telli nun.

ADA. Fani tay lakshi ma tay kani bo, la bo kani lakshi ma
ma kati tay.

> (TOM *looks up again, his voice rising in intensity.*
> ADA*'s voice rises as well.)*

TOM. Stani kay ma, / stani kay ma lani bo no cha dee, bo lana fa keesho ba tee orati nah, mana kay lah fah neesh taba so mana tay! *Keli kay kana toh, kana toh lah –*

ADA. / Oh nee kaga bashi, bashi la toni ma, toni ma la kani ba sho do legi fa! Bashi nah, fo lah toh seti nah! Akna folo toto bani kah fee! Kah fee!

MARCUS. *Jesus Lord God Jesus Praise Him* / ola bana ola tor vishi lado ma tei, ola gana fa Jesus God Lord Jesus Bless Me Jesus Christ Bless Me gana fo la bi neenee.

JOSH. / Ton aba la shinee fo na elli gay ma sha ta no, sha to no la fia donono, tona! Gona may finay ma la gona fa to la!

DENISE. Doni fa ma lana kay ta, lana kay ta bishee nay. Bilee ma fa nini konana, konana tana binee kay tona la ba ma!

> (**JOSH** *kneels down on the floor. Everyone is now speaking at once, slowly rising in volume.*)

ADA. / Tona bee ma doni ka lee, foto ba moshi kay too. Alla too ma teha bay, la goro isha ba ma toni bee ma doni. Toni be ma doni, doni ma doni la too teha by. Ish ba laktha da, coli la ba toni baba, ishi ma taka bra, coli fa sili dada. Toni ba leekhi vaba da, toni da. Ora ta she tay, kun ska la tor, bora ra koosh, la dora kanar dee ban too la beya tone ta, for a tan do mo shrona ka fa. Fola kora tee, kora tee no tando fay. Oraka mash foret kali, kali beh no rona fornat ka, fornat ka ola tandora me. Me lora fa tee, fa tee –

TOM. / Cani ba ti ma, ba ti man elish man sho tee mon àla kee shina ba. Shin aba mon tona, tona cala bon shimi, cono ta. Cono ta mani. Praise you O Lord God, praise you. Roya ma taya naj ala taya, ay ya shila boy coy a titi a titi a nani, caraya loya a boreah, no shonda fan ti, fan ti, no shona fan ti dora leeni fanak. O Lord God praise, oranti fineesh, korash feeni alat ka, mora ta loma fan do, fan do loma! Korana nash ta foret ali yo, gora lash rana manto barata shanti, shanti, forana ka lee –!

MARCUS. / Sar deyu yet bee naru Jesus Lord God, sar de biki dora, ora bish kesh kedet Lord God Jesus, Lord Jesus God bless me Lord God, so sevu parde na la lang bet mani kay la, Lord Jesus bless me Lord Jesus God, alla kan da ma kin do, Lord Jesus, Lord Jesus God, alla nan kani bo, kani lan tee dora fasha se, alla man bet arak! Kora shan for arana nuta erer, tre shora bo Jesus God bless me Jesus God bless me Lord! Arana fan deelo fosh rona fan, amaka bo loke, bo loke Jesus God Bless me Jesus, bora kasha lak Jesus God –!

DENISE. *(Slightly slower than the rest.)* / Rohoosh dan elay, gona ta day elli bay no bo no shona kay la bosh ell con te man be al aba tona bay ma bee. Tona ma bay mee tona. Tona ma bay elli con mosho. Elli con mosho bora fana ta lee. Forak alla, borna me conte mana ta rash fa lo. Ta rash fa lo, orak ma tee. Fanate do. Ora mandata lay, torosh a koni tay.

JOSH. Ko ra shana fo rata, a shana bora ma ka. Bora ma ka, Jesus God, bora ma ka. Eli sonna kora ta ta, bela ma rasha fata lata, Kora ma shana la ta, Jesus fora sha laka ta, fora ana resh sha ita ma ro kana ma. Kana ma ro lata. Kana ma ro lata shay, yah showya yana dala God, Jesus oh yah por sum del akna kitte maseen shoya kah. Alana rashna, mashadele showa lo seya kan da, kando foyet! Foyet mastica foresh ta la, bora tama ke rana maseyah, kolesh ta beesh femi, alak ana! Foresh ta, alak ana!

> *(Everyone continues to rise in volume.* **ADA** *and* **MARCUS** *start moving around the space.* **TOM** *slowly becomes overcome with emotion.)*

ADA. / Toni ba ba no, toni la coli sho ifa la bish kan! Tona ba shini dolo nana, coma toda fo. Kora toda fasha to, fasha to ray masha ka leya fora toh, mora taka falana nashti, nashti mona nash arak, avala lak! Avala lak toh ray, wala pa do kora tah fay! Elli kay! Elli kay! Cola shodo fishi ma did fata, ma did fata co lono, kan dori ma fola tan, ana fashti solan aka! Effi see! Effi see kolo!

Co lono a fidi tata, ele kama, ele biti, ele con to. Elli con to! Elli con to!

TOM. / Naj a la borea, ay ya boreata, shila a boreata, a loya a roya, a kiti ma, naja a borea la a titi yah, a loya a roya, praise you God, please lord God, et ta kish ka leda, para do la, doh die! Mana ka la biki! Mana ka la oresh ta mini fa, fatuah adoni elihulu, elihulu O please Lord God, please ma shoni foh eli bara tun redna wan forna lan voni mosh borek mana con vonta moreni bona lee, bona lee wosh rana do foreshi kan la zan! Korsa nam yuno God, please O Lord mana la biki O Lord!

MARCUS. / Son aba alla kan min kin go O Jesus Lord God, tana min sono ba mi, sono ba mi! Elle kan do mishi lan bin to mana kin do, mana kin do! O Lord Jesus God bless me, bless me O Lord Jesus God, mana kin do! Mana kin do, O Lord Jesus God, O bless me! Korna fana al kan gona vishna, allat ma kan, allat ma kan Jesus O God Lord Jesus! Bora ta dorana van dee, van de dorana nomo ranata Jesus God kora donu pishma, pishma for nak, for nak! Pishma lana O Jesus God bless me God!

DENISE. / Mono ta ra fana tata, eli ka ma. Eli tash roma, eli mana faraka. Oni may fara tosh bana. Tosh bana ra kanana. Ay ero mai, how ma yeavu, how ma kai nini! Yeavu nishni yoma na, yinto dishi fana tata, eli kay ma! Voni to do lora, boki manta mishi loka fora ta bo! Kana may kandee, kandee lash beni mo, lash beni mo, lash beni mo! Kora fo!

JOSH. A rona kando, a li ka lolo, a ki sundi mosh roshi Jesus God, spirit Jesus God spirit a roshi ma lani fora tash tama. Tama lay no, for manash a ko, spirit Jesus manush tee fola, vona manashti, spirit Lord arasah ta bee! Yo no fola kana terishi mana, mana bo karash ta bee, eli suk! Eli suk vora ray tee mo, ray tee sura dasha fing nah! Spirit Lord, fora tash tama Jesus fora tash, ala kara tam tara, ala kra aresh mama tora alana, alik karem shatay, *alik karem shorat ata, neba suruk!*

(**JOSH** *lies down on the floor, facing up.* **TOM** *lifts his hands to the air, nearly weeping.* **ADA** *begins to frantically circle the room.* **MARCUS** *stomps his feet, punctuating his speech.*)

(**DENISE** *moves to a corner, concentrating on her speech. Everyone's volume slowly rises to a shout.*)

ADA. / Miki ba no sho, *elli kan to! Elli kan to!* MA BA DONA FA TEE, ELLISH MATA FONO BA NONO, CAMA TAN TELIKA COMO TAN DO, MANASH TATA BO TANKI BAN KELLI BAN SHEE, BAN SHEE BO KANA TAN DEE! BAN SHEE BO KANA TAN DEE! TAN DEE! ARASHA BAN ALA KANA, KANA TO MANASH BORA FAH OLA, OLA MAKA TIRIKA MOSHTA! KALA TEE! KALA TEE! ORA FORESHI TINAH VAN KAH! *TINAAAAAHHHHH!* Tinah van kah! Tan dee – …

TOM. / TONA A ROY, TONA A ROY! ANA MA SAR A BIKI DORDA! SKINA A BOYETU, RAY A BISH MANA KARA! A DORRA! ROHU KISH KAMA SON O LORD! O LORD GOD O PRAISE HIM LORD O PRAISE HIM KANA MISH KANA! MISH KANA! O LORD GOD PRAISE HIM JESUS ANA FOLANA TASH NEE, BORAK A TEENO MOSH GORA TABNAH! TABNAH GAN MANA POLOSH INNI FON DORI! CANA, POR KAY TORO!

MARCUS. / BLESS ME GOD JESUS LORD, LORD JESUS GOD BLESS ME KANA BIN RATA LA, KANA BIN RATA MIN LORD GOD JESUS BLESS ME, O LORD GOD JESUS BLESS ME KANA RIN A TANA MA! A TANA MA LORD JESUS GOD BLESS ME! KANA DO! KANA DO LORD JESUS GOD BLESS ME ALIKA RONATA ZEEN KANAF, KANAFTA BASHTEE FON RONO SHEEK BELI KAH! BELI KAH BORAH, O JESUS GOD! *Jesus Lord bless me borah ka beli, beli kah* – …

DENISE. / Dona Ka! Dona ka lima bana! BANA LA TEE! BANA LA TEE KO, KO MO SHAMA VENI LA TANA! VENI –, ELISH PORA KA LA FA NANA. FORNA KORING DOH, LAKA MANEESH! MANEESH IDISH BODO ZAN SEE, ALEK AVASHNA! MAN SURA

BANTEE, BANAKA LASH O YONO BANAKA NA!
BANAKA NAH ALEE TASH DEE!

JOSH. NEBA SURUK! SURUK OLA KA MORA SHOSH,
ARUSH TOMA, ARUSH TOMA! FONO KA LO, A
FONO KA LO! ARUSH TOMA FONO KA LO! KA LO!
BANASH FEE MO JESUS LORD, ZOK DONOSHO
BOK AMASHTI LAY BORI NO! SPIRIT O LORD
JESUS KANASH TEE BEE! AMAKA LEE ASHNO GO
MORA FA TEE LO, A GALAKA MOSHTI VANUSH,
ALA FEEN DEE DO FARUSH... Farush a no... Farush
a no... O Lord, I pray... I pray to you O Lord...

> (JOSH *stops, takes deep breaths in and out.*
> *Everyone begins to calm down a bit.* TOM *slowly*
> *lowers his arms.*)

ADA. / ...tan dee, cana. Tele ma shimi to mash... Shimi rez
mana ta bo lala... Shono kan... Bensh man tati. Bensch
man tati... Man tati... In Lord Jesus' name, Amen.

TOM. / PRAISE HIM KORA POR KAY TORO. PRAISE
HIM JESUS KORA TANA, kora tana... Kora forat
shtaba a raka ta, a raka ta ma, praise him Jesus O praise
him, kora tana bata... Arasha ma min akata. Arahsa,
Jesus God.

MARCUS. / ...O Lord Jesus God bless me... Kana la bin ana
tana, Lord Jesus God bless me a ey ma... Ma rey taka di
sho Lord Jesus... Lord Jesus bless me... A kan tini ma,
Lord Jesus bless me, kana rin ma shi...

DENISE. BARA FA LA MANA. Mana ka la sha. Pora tana
la tash ala, boru fama shana ta ada... Fora ma laka
shata... Ora kama...

> (*Slowly,* ADA *finishes, opening her eyes. She takes*
> *a deep breath, looks around the room.* MARCUS,
> TOM, *and* DENISE *begin to slow down, their*
> *volume decreasing.* JOSH *stares up at the ceiling,*
> *motionless.*)

TOM. / Kora fana taba sha tata, Jesus God. O Jesus Lord
fara tanash, for a masha lata koresh a mana, mana fa
lata bata, oreshi manuk, oreshi manuk Jesus Lord.

DENISE. / Ana ba loshi a kara ta mi… Aleshi mora bama toh kana na… In Christ's name I pray to you Lord Jesus. Amen.

MARCUS. O Lord God bless me Jesus Lord God… Shana bin ma ra tin, shana bin ra… Jesus Lord, God… O Lord Jesus bless me. Kana rin ma Jesus Lord… Jesus, Jesus Lord… Jesus Lord. Amen.

> (**MARCUS** *opens his eyes, goes to* **DENISE**. *He wraps his arms around her.* **DENISE** *smiles at him a bit, then gently pushes him off.*)

(Soft.) What?

TOM. / Foresh ala tana… Jesus, Lord Jesus… Fa nana toreki ma… Ma…

DENISE. *(Soft.)* Nothing, shh.

> (*Silence. Everyone breathes in and out.*)

ADA. Okay guys, / let's –

TOM. In Jesus' name, Amen.

> (**TOM** *takes a breath, then opens his eyes, looking at* **ADA**. *He mouths "sorry,"* **ADA** *smiles at him.*)
>
> (**JOSH** *looks at* **TOM**, **TOM** *averts his eyes from him.*)
>
> (**ADA** *goes to the kitchenette, takes her Starbucks cup, taking a long drink.*)

ADA. Okay.

> (*Pause.*)

Okay let's regroup!

Shortly Later.

(MICHAELA *stands at the base of the stairs wearing a ratty t-shirt and unwashed jeans. She looks at* JOSH, *who stands on the other side of the room, looking back at her.* ADA *stands awkwardly between them.*)

(*A strange silence.*)

ADA. (*To* MICHAELA.) Well.

(*Short pause.*)

My condolences.

MICHAELA. C'mon, Ada.

(*Another strange silence. Finally,* ADA *exits up the stairs.*)

JOSH. You shouldn't have come.

MICHAELA. You wouldn't answer your phone, what the hell else was I supposed to do?

(*Pause.*)

When are you leaving?

JOSH. Three days.

MICHAELA. *Three –?*

(*Pause.*)

How long are you –? I mean when are you planning on coming back?

JOSH. Right now – I'm not planning on coming back.

(*Then, from upstairs, we hear the sound of a choir singing "Nearer, My God, To Thee," shrill and off-key.*)

MICHAELA. How long have you been planning to do this?

JOSH. A long time, Mickey.

MICHAELA. So you're all just –? All of you are just *moving to the Middle East?*

JOSH. Everyone else is going for four months, that was the original plan for the mission. But I've thought about it, and I just – decided I could do more.

MICHAELA. You mean throw your whole life away.

JOSH. Okay, if you want to talk about this rationally, / we can –

MICHAELA. You could've –, you know, *kept me in the loop* about this –

JOSH. That's why I emailed you.

MICHAELA. A three sentence email sent four days before you move across the planet isn't keeping me in the loop, it's a fucking suicide note.

JOSH. Oh just stop it, Mickey –

MICHAELA. You don't know anything about the Middle East.

JOSH. I've been training for over a year, / I'm ready for this –

MICHAELA. You can't just waltz in there with your Bibles and expect everyone to / welcome you with open –

JOSH. It's not –. It's not just about evangelism, it's about working at schools, hospitals – I'll be in a more rural area so / there's plenty of –

MICHAELA. Well, you're not going. You're being crazy, and I'm telling you that you're not doing this.

(Pause. JOSH heads toward the stairs.)

JOSH. Okay, I need to go to work, we can talk about / this later –

MICHAELA. Is this some kind of – mental breakdown, should I be worried?

(JOSH turns back to her.)

JOSH. What is so hard to understand about this?! Plenty of people spend their lives doing this!

MICHAELA. Crazy people, Josh! Crazy people spend / their lives doing this!

JOSH. Alright I'm not having this discussion with you right now, you're being totally disrespectful, it's impossible to / talk to you when you're like this –

MICHAELA. Obviously I had no idea how far you had gone with this stuff, if I knew that you were ready to do something this stupid I would have come back a long time ago –

JOSH. *No. You wouldn't have.*

     (Pause.)

MICHAELA. Is this about Dad? Is that what's going on?

JOSH. No, this has / nothing to do –

MICHAELA. I'm sorry I wasn't here, Josh.

JOSH. I don't care.

MICHAELA. I know I should have been here to help with everything, but that / doesn't mean –

JOSH. *I didn't need your help.* I handled the burial, the house, everything. I didn't need you. So you don't get to suddenly waltz in here three weeks after he dies and act like you have any authority over me at all.

     *(Pause. They stare at one another. The choir continues to sing. **JOSH** and **MICHAELA** begin to calm down.)*

MICHAELA. I'm sorry.

     (Pause.)

   Jesus.

JOSH. Don't – …

     *(Pause. **MICHAELA** outstretches her arms for a hug. **JOSH** relents, goes to her, embraces her.)*

MICHAELA. It's good to see you.

JOSH. It's good to see you, too.

     (Pause.)

   You sort of –

MICHAELA. I stink, I know. I've been in the car for like thirteen hours.

>*(They release each other but remain close. Pause.)*

JOSH. Are you still –? The group home thing?

MICHAELA. No actually. Have my own place, couple years now. Little studio, it's –. It's fine. Better than the group home.

>*(Pause.)*

JOSH. Are you –?

MICHAELA. *Yes*, Josh, I –. I've been clean for four years. You know that.

JOSH. That's good.

>*(Pause. **JOSH** goes to the kitchenette, filling an electric kettle with water.)*

MICHAELA. *(Re: the choir.)* They sound terrible.

JOSH. Yeah.

MICHAELA. I thought –. You told me you were the choir director?

JOSH. That was years ago. Didn't last very long.

MICHAELA. What happened?

JOSH. I don't know, it was just a disaster. I told Mrs. Askins that she should consider toning down her vibrato and she looked at me like she was gonna punch me in the throat. They got Sandy Hutchins to lead the choir now.

MICHAELA. Sandy Hutchins? Like near the mall Hutchins?

JOSH. Yeah.

MICHAELA. I thought they were Mormon.

JOSH. You think everyone in Idaho Falls is Mormon.

MICHAELA. Well almost everyone is.

>*(Pause. **MICHAELA** spies a pile of brochures, she picks one up. The choir upstairs finishes.)*

"He is coming, and soon. Will you be a warrior?"

JOSH. Mickey.

MICHAELA. *(Reading.)* "Two millennia ago, God sent his only begotten son to free us from the confines of this earthly life. Some have received his message. And fewer still have been called to spread his message throughout the globe."

JOSH. *Mickey.*

MICHAELA. "Christ's message in the third world is a seedling struggling toward the sun – will you help to water its roots?"

> *(Stops reading.)*

Wow.

JOSH. The church didn't write that, this is from a group that's sponsoring the mission, it's not / even –

MICHAELA. I mean – you have better *taste* than this. Right?

> *(**JOSH** gives her a look. Pause.)*

Look, Josh, I know what this is, I ran away from Idaho Falls too, I know what you're doing. But you can't –

JOSH. I'm not *running away,* I – ...

> *(Pause.)*

Mickey, I have the chance to do something really *good* here, you know? These people are suffering – suffering more than you and I ever did. I have the opportunity to really *commit* to helping them. Not just for four months, but for my whole *life.* It's –

> *(The electric kettle begins to whistle. **JOSH** goes to it, unplugs it, opens the lid off a cup of ramen noodles, pours the boiling water into it.)*

I just want to help people. That's what I want to do with my life. Just – help.

> *(Pause.)*

MICHAELA. By saving their souls.

> *(**JOSH** looks at her. **ADA** re-enters.)*

ADA. I'm sorry to interrupt. I just need the recorders.

> (**ADA** *points to a tub full of plastic recorders.* **ADA** *goes to it, picks it up.*)
>
> (**ADA** *looks at* **JOSH**.)

ADA. You okay?

JOSH. Yeah.

> (*Pause.*)

ADA. You sure?

> (**MICHAELA** *looks at* **ADA** *quizzically.*)

JOSH. Yeah, really. Thanks, Ada.

> (**ADA** *smiles at both of them, heads back upstairs.* **MICHAELA** *watches her go, then turns to* **JOSH**.)

MICHAELA. What the hell was that?

JOSH. Don't worry about it.

MICHAELA. Okay, I can't be here anymore, can we please go back to the house?

JOSH. You can, but I have to go work. Are you staying the night?

> (**JOSH** *grabs his cup of noodles and a plastic fork.*)

MICHAELA. Yeah.

JOSH. There's a key behind the rain barrel near the barn.

MICHAELA. I remember.

> (**JOSH** *finds his backpack, gets ready to leave.* **MICHAELA** *goes to him.*)

Josh.

> (*Pause.* **JOSH** *looks at her.*)

You don't have to move halfway around the world, Dad's *gone.* And I'm sorry for being a shit sister, I'm sorry for not being here for you when he died, but things haven't exactly been easy for me either, and – …

> (*Pause.*)

Please, just – *don't do this.*

(Pause. **JOSH** *looks at her.)*

*(***ADA** *re-enters, busying herself with some boxes. She
mouths "sorry" to* **JOSH** *and* **MICHAELA**.*)*

JOSH. I have work.

*(***JOSH** *exits up the stairs.)*

*(***ADA** *smiles at* **MICHAELA**, *goes to her.)*

ADA. You know if you had any questions about the mission
itself, I'd be / happy to –

MICHAELA. You can't possibly let him do this.

*(***ADA** *smiles at her.)*

ADA. Michaela, I *hear* you.

MICHAELA. Okay.

ADA. I *really do.*

MICHAELA. Thanks.

ADA. And believe me – I reacted the same way, I told him
he was moving too quickly, he should just do the four
month mission with the rest of us, but –. He's adamant.
And, honestly, if this is how he chooses to deal with
your dad's death, by devoting the rest of his life to
saving others – how can I stand in judgment of that?

*(Pause. Then, from upstairs, we hear the sound of
dozens of recorders playing an off-key version of "A
Mighty Fortress Is Our God.")*

He'll have *plenty* of support, believe me. From what
I hear the village they're placing him in is *really*
interesting, and there are a few other people from the
Evangelical Church League living there –

MICHAELA. Wait, so – you guys aren't going to be with him
at all?

ADA. Michaela, he'll have plenty of support.

(Awkward pause. The music upstairs stops.)

So how are you doing anyway?!

(Pause.)

MICHAELA. I'm fine.

ADA. You ended up moving to – Eugene, is that right?

MICHAELA. Yep.

>   *(Pause.)*

ADA. So what brought you to Eugene?

MICHAELA. The meth.

>   *(The music upstairs resumes – even louder and more off-key than before.)*

Early Evening.

(JOSH, ADA, TOM, DENISE, *and* MARCUS *all sit in folding chairs.* MARCUS *is addressing* JOSH, *nervous. Everyone but* ADA *holds a textbook in beginning Arabic.*)

MARCUS. Ana ismee Marcus. Eye-na esemek? [My name is Marcus. Where is your name?]

ADA. Ma esemek. [What is your name.]

MARCUS. Ma esemek. Crap. Sorry.

ADA. La mooshkele! [No problem!]

MARCUS. Ana ismee Marcus. Ma esemek?

JOSH. Isem Josh. Ana min Am-ree-kah, min waleya Idaho. Medina tesme Idaho Falls. Awad an attah-hud-athe alaye-koom ayn yay-sooah. [My name is Josh. I am from America, from the state Idaho. A city called Idaho Falls. I would like to talk to you about Jesus.]

(*Pause.*)

MARCUS. (*A stab in the dark.*) Yes.

(*Pause.*)

ADA. Okay this is good! Mumtez! [Excellent!] You're engaging them, looking them in the eye, that's great. Half of communication is just the confidence of looking someone right in the eye, that's something I learned really quickly when I was over there. So – Josh just told you that he'd like to talk to you about Jesus, did you get that?

MARCUS. Yeah! Totally, I think so.

ADA. Okay great! So do you want to try to ask Josh the same thing?

MARCUS. Yeah totally.

(MARCUS *looks back to* JOSH.)

Hal too-reed – ...al-kee-tall an... Jesus?

ADA. Okay good! But you just asked him if he wanted to fight about Jesus.

MARCUS. *(Defeated.)* I am *such an idiot* with this stuff.

       (**DENISE** *comforts him.*)

DENISE. Marcus, honey, you have come *so far* with this.

MARCUS. No I haven't.

DENISE. You have! You couldn't even count in Arabic two months ago!

MARCUS. Babe, I *still* get seven and eight mixed up, and –

ADA. Marcus, look, if language isn't your thing, that's not a big deal. Like we keep saying, you're gonna meet a *ton* of people who already speak English, there's plenty of work for you to be doing.

MARCUS. No, I know, I just – … It's not that. It's just I get worried that if I'm somewhere where I can't find you guys, and I need help / or something, and –

ADA. / That won't happen!

DENISE. Honey, it's fine!

MARCUS. I *know*, I talk about this every week and I'm sure you guys are sick of it, but I just – … I'm just nervous.

TOM. I mean it's probably good.

       (Pause.)

MARCUS. What?

TOM. I mean you should be nervous. It is dangerous over there, it's good that you're nervous. They had two revolutions in the last decade, it's dangerous. So maybe being nervous is good.

       (Awkward silence.)

ADA. Yeah I think there's a lot of things about what Tom is saying that are right! I think some nerves are healthy!

DENISE. That's true.

TOM. Because it's really dangerous over there.

ADA. Sure, but –. We're only gonna be there for four months, so I wouldn't –

TOM. Not all of us.

> **(JOSH** *looks at* **TOM. TOM** *doesn't look back.)*
>
> *(Pause.)*

ADA. Here's the thing though – I know this is going to
sound sort of crazy, but with all that going on? It almost
makes it feel like – God is *there.* He's waiting for these
people to come to him.

> *(Pause.)*

I haven't told you guys this story yet because it's sort of
personal, but. I mean like I said when I was there last
year it was mostly training and junk, I didn't do a ton of
witnessing. But there was this one night, I just felt the
spirit inside of me tell me to *go.* And so I start walking,
and I head into this part of town that's really not that
safe, and – by the way, *do not* do this you guys – I was
walking down this street and I sort of hear this voice in
me go – *stop.* So I stopped, and I looked around, and
there was this woman standing there, and I'm pretty
sure she was a prostitute? And she looked at me, and
/ she said –

DENISE. Wow, how'd you know she was a prostitute?

ADA. She just – …

> *(Pause.)*

Anyway she looks at me and she says to me: "Something
inside me told me I would meet you here tonight."

MARCUS. / That is *awesome* –

DENISE. / Oh, wow.

JOSH. That's amazing.

ADA. *Yes.*

> *(Pause.)*

So I sat down with her, and we probably talked for two
hours or so. And at the end of the conversation, we
prayed right there, together, on the street, as the sun
was coming up and we could hear all the calls to prayer
from all the different mosques in the distance.

DENISE. / That's so, so beautiful.

MARCUS. / *Awesome.*

JOSH. Wow.

ADA. I mean it was one of those moments where you really feel like God just – *showed up.* You just sort of follow the voice, you follow Him, and He'll appear in your life when you least expect it.

> *(Pause.)*

But I mean of course – they don't all work out like that.

JOSH. / Oh sure.

MARCUS. / Totally.

DENISE. Yeah.

ADA. But I really hope that you guys have an experience like that. I *know* you will. It might not be as dramatic, it might be totally different, but I just know – God's going to show up for you. He will.

> *(Pause. **ADA** takes a drink from her Starbucks cup.)*

MARCUS. But like when you were there, was there like – gunfire, or –?

ADA. *(Re: the coffee.)* Oo, they didn't make this right.

> *(To the group.)*

How about let's do some Arabic Pictionary.

Night.

(The church is empty and dark.)

(JOSH, alone, sits at the piano, ear buds in his ears. He stares at the piano in silence.)

(After a moment, TOM comes down the stairs, holding a bag full of groceries. JOSH doesn't hear him.)

TOM. Josh.

(JOSH still doesn't hear. TOM goes to him, JOSH doesn't move.)

Josh.

(TOM puts a hand on his shoulder. JOSH turns around, startled.)

JOSH. *Oh* –

TOM. Sorry, sorry –

JOSH. No, it's –. It's okay.

(Pause.)

Hi.

TOM. Hi.

(Pause.)

What're you listening to?

JOSH. *(Holding up his phone.)* It's – Brahms. "Requiem."

TOM. It's okay.

JOSH. There's some really beautiful passages.

TOM. Fauré's is better.

(Pause. They look at each other.)

JOSH. I'm glad you came.

(Pause. TOM extends the bag.)

TOM. I got you some stuff.

(JOSH takes the bag, looking inside.)

JOSH. Maple bars?

TOM. They're day-old.

JOSH. That's fine.

TOM. Maybe two actually. Have some fruit first.

> (**TOM** *takes out some of the groceries, putting them in the kitchenette.*)

JOSH. You didn't have to do this.

TOM. You have to eat something other than ramen.

> (**JOSH** *smiles at* **TOM**. *He takes out the maple bars.*)

JOSH. I'm – glad you're talking to me, I was worried you wouldn't say anything to me ever again.

TOM. I don't have that much self-control, even a week was like impossible for me. Oh my gosh, eat an orange first, you're gonna get scurvy or something.

> (**JOSH** *smiles, takes out an orange.*)

JOSH. Are you still mad at me for deciding to move over there, or –?

TOM. I'm not mad, Josh, I just –. Gotta get used to not being able to talk to you, I guess.

JOSH. We'll still talk.

TOM. You know what I mean.

> (*Pause.*)

When I get back from the mission and you won't be here – I don't know. I feel like it's just gonna be me, alone in this town with my dad, and whenever I get thinking about it, I just – … It doesn't make me feel good.

JOSH. You could think about leaving. That music program at OU, the one you were looking at a few months ago?

> (**TOM** *looks away, finishes putting away the groceries.*)

TOM. C'mon. That's never gonna happen.

JOSH. If you can't do out-of-state tuition, you could look at Boise State, or –

TOM. Josh, I've never lived anywhere else, I don't know if I could ever – …

    (Pause.)

Also, my dad, he –. He tries so hard with me, and if I left he'd be all alone, I just –.

    (Pause. **TOM** *sits with him.)*

JOSH. Oh wait, I didn't tell you –

TOM. What?

    (**JOSH** *grabs his backpack, opening it up.)*

JOSH. I was packing up a couple days ago, and I found these…

    (**JOSH** *pulls out a small stack of CDs.* **TOM** *recognizes them immediately.)*

TOM. *(Mortified.)* No. *Why do you have those?*

JOSH. I don't know, you must have left them over at my house or something –

TOM. Okay, we are getting rid of them *right now* –

JOSH. I can't believe what you listened to before we became friends. Do you realize there is an *Ashlee Simpson* single in here?!

TOM. I was like twelve years old!

    (**TOM** *tries to take the CDs away from* **JOSH**. **JOSH** *pulls them away playfully.)*

JOSH. No, I wanna take them with me!

TOM. It's so embarrassing.

JOSH. No, it's not, it's –.

    (Short pause, looking at the CDs.)

I just think it's funny.

    (Pause.)

TOM. I went up to the golf course last night without you, it was weird.

JOSH. Did you get caught?

TOM. Almost. New groundskeeper is such a jerk.

>   *(Short pause.)*

I went up to the top of the hill, the third hole.

JOSH. Fourth.

TOM. No it's not.

JOSH. Third hole is the one by the highway, then up the /
hill the –

TOM. *Anyway.* I was wondering if I could see your house
from up there. Like if I could just find the little red
light on top of the water tower near your place, but
there was no way, it was too far off and it was about to
rain, and –.

>   *(Pause.)*

Started feeling like I didn't even know what direction I
was facing. Like I didn't recognize anything, the whole
town was just – ...

>   *(**TOM** looks down. Pause.)*

JOSH. Are you –? Have you had any anxiety attacks this
week?

TOM. I'm fine.

JOSH. Tom, you can tell me, / I –

TOM. I'm just –. It's not a big deal, it's just been once or
twice, and they haven't been bad, I haven't thrown up
or anything, I...

>   *(Pause.)*

I actually – tried talking with my dad about it.

JOSH. Really?

TOM. Yeah.

>   *(Pause.)*

JOSH. Has he – helped?

TOM. I guess? His big thing is that I can find comfort in
prayer, which is right. I can. Pretty much the only time
I'm not anxious about something. But I try to tell him
it's more complicated than that, I get anxious all the

time, I never know how to calm myself down, and he just –. He doesn't get it. I can tell he doesn't know what to say, so he just keeps telling me to pray. That if my mom were still alive she would just tell me to pray on it.

(Short pause.)

Truth is, she probably wouldn't say anything, she'd just – listen to me.

(Pause.)

(JOSH *reaches for his headphones.)*

JOSH. Here, listen to this.

TOM. Nah –

JOSH. Seriously just listen, I just like stumbled on it earlier today, it's Wagner, it's the / prelude to –

TOM. Wagner nooooooo –

JOSH. *You'll like this one.* Stop.

> **(JOSH** *puts one earbud in his ear, hands the other one to* **TOM**. **TOM** *doesn't put it in his ear.* **JOSH** *scrolls through his phone.)*

It's the prelude to this opera, "Das…rain-gold?" I don't know, anyway –

TOM. Josh –

JOSH. Just listen – it's like one, big, huge crescendo of the same chord for like *four minutes,* I'd never really –

TOM. *I don't –* …

> **(TOM** *drops the earbud, standing up, facing away from* **JOSH**.*)*
>
> *(Pause.)*

JOSH. I'm sorry –

TOM. It's fine, I – …

> **(JOSH** *stops the music, takes out the earbud. Pause.)*

JOSH. Tom, can't we just – …? We only have a couple days, can we just – be normal?

(Pause. **TOM** *doesn't look at him.)*

TOM. Have you found a place to live yet?

(Pause.)

JOSH. You really want to know?

TOM. I'm just wondering.

(Pause.)

JOSH. Yeah, they – … The ECL people helped me find a place. An apartment in the middle of the village, not too far from a couple other missionaries that have been there for a few years.

(Pause. **TOM** *still doesn't look at him.)*

TOM. When I get back – I'm gonna rot here.

JOSH. Don't say that –

TOM. It's the truth.

JOSH. You're going to be *fine*, we're both going to be –

TOM. I was at work earlier today and a woman came up to me and asked me some question, something about glossy paper, or –. And I looked up from my register, and I see her, and suddenly in my head I'm like – I'm going to die before my shift is over. Like – this is a fact, this is something that is going to happen to me before I leave work today. And I helped the woman, I led her through the store and I'm thinking – I'm going to die today. And I showed her the paper, I recommended the ultra-glossy, I went back to my register, I kept working, and all the time I'm thinking – I'm going to die today. But then I finish out the rest of my shift, I clocked out, went back to my car, and suddenly I was like – oh. I'm *not* going to die today.

(Pause. Then, **TOM** *becomes overwhelmed. He looks away from* **JOSH**.*)*

JOSH. Hey –

TOM. I'm fine.

JOSH. Here, let's –. Pray with me.

(**JOSH** *goes to him.*)

Let's just – pray. We can do that, that'll help. Right?

(*They look at each other for a moment. Finally,* **JOSH** *closes his eyes.*)

(*Silence.*)

(*Softly.*)

Lord, please help us. Please come into our hearts, please calm us, please let us take comfort in your spirit, please...

(*Pause.*)

Kana lo mee... Kala po shana mafa to...

(**TOM** *closes his eyes, joining him.*)

TOM. / No hana mee. Ko fana tay folo ja, een ma neeno folo ba. Ko lana fa ta, oresh bana ama, fanish ko tala dee. Oreni ma ya washa voto, korna fana.

JOSH. Elee go roh, toba tani ma. Toba tani ma fa rashi go fa mo. Yola bata towa nak, ulu pon mosha do fara ret, fara ret an donacha man nami kai fana shto.

(**MICHAELA** *appears at the top of the stairs. She descends a step or two, watching them.*)

TOM. / Folo ba ma tora dono ta. Dono lana poleshi fan do, wona fanak ee tay shosh weli ba. Ola man tee, bora ta.

JOSH. Fora mani kay shoraba kalee, malle manashta prati lo tona, alle yan kanti may no tandi ma kay, kolee bor anna mah –

(**TOM** *hears someone, stops, and looks up.* **JOSH** *stops as well, sees* **MICHAELA**. *A tense pause.*)

MICHAELA. Hi.

(*Pause.*)

TOM. (*Recognizing her.*) Michaela?

MICHAELA. Yeah. Hey, Tom.

TOM. I didn't know – ... I didn't know you were in town.

MICHAELA. Josh sent me an email yesterday. Figured it was time for a visit.

(*Pause.* **TOM** *heads toward the exit.*)

TOM. I'll let you / guys –

MICHAELA. I don't mean / to –

TOM. It's fine, I should head home anyway.

(**MICHAELA** *smiles at* **TOM**, *he heads up the stairs and exits.*)

(*Silence.*)

MICHAELA. I waited at the house for a while, went by the car wash, they said you got off hours ago. Figured you were here.

(*Pause.*)

Josh, what –? What was that?

(*Pause.* **JOSH** *looks away.*)

JOSH. It's just praying.

(*Pause.*)

MICHAELA. But what –? I don't understand, what language was that, what / was –?

JOSH. It's not a language, it – … It's not a big deal, we were just praying in tongues.

MICHAELA. "Tongues?" Like – gibberish?

JOSH. It's just – sometimes it's nice to pray, to focus on something, but there's not the pressure of making *sense*, or…

(*Pause.*)

It just – helps.

(*Pause.*)

MICHAELA. I just don't understand / why –

JOSH. I don't think that like, God is talking through me or anything, it's just a way to relax and connect with something larger.

(Short pause.)

It just sort of – comes to you. You just close your eyes and start talking, and just...

(**JOSH** *trails off, looking away. Pause.*)

MICHAELA. I'm sorry, it's just – *really weird* –

JOSH. Okay, I'm not going to apologize for what I believe, or how I believe it.

MICHAELA. I don't want you to apologize, I'm just / trying to –

JOSH. Don't you ever want to believe in something bigger than yourself?

(Pause. **MICHAELA** *looks at him.)*

MICHAELA. You're right, I –. I'm sorry.

(Pause.)

I'm just – not used to all this, it's –. Sorry.

(Pause. **JOSH** *softens.)*

So, you –. What time are you supposed to leave on Friday?

(**JOSH** *looks at her.*)

I'm not –. I'm just asking.

(Short pause.)

JOSH. Morning. Pretty early.

(Pause.)

MICHAELA. I can't believe you've been taking orders from Ada.

JOSH. I mean, I won't be much longer. They're all staying in the capital, but as soon as I get there I take a ten-hour bus ride up into the mountains. A little village.

MICHAELA. What are you planning on – doing there?

JOSH. There's a lot I can do. There's a school there that burned down a few years ago, there are some missionaries working to rebuild it. Teach English, work with kids. I can do – a lot of good, I think.

(Pause.)

JOSH. I think I'm gonna be happy there, Mickey. Really.

(Silence.)

MICHAELA. Josh, there was –. The tent, set up in the back yard? With the camping stove, tons of empty propane canisters, empty ramen packages everywhere?

> *(Pause.* **JOSH** *goes to the kitchenette, takes the electric kettle, fills it with water.)*

JOSH. I just sleep out there sometimes.

(Pause.)

MICHAELA. And to be honest when I was going through the house it almost looked like nothing had been touched in weeks, a layer of dust over all the cups in the kitchen / and –

JOSH. Why didn't you come as soon as I told you that Dad died?

(Pause.)

MICHAELA. Josh –

JOSH. No, I'm serious. Don't act like I'm the only one who needs to explain some stuff.

(Pause.)

MICHAELA. I was in the car. I was all packed. And – I never left the parking lot at my apartment.

(Pause.)

I kept thinking about you, out here, dealing with this on your own, and I kept telling myself that I *had to go*, but… Then I'd think about Dad. I'd think about him lying in that coffin or whatever, I'd think about having to see his body, and I – couldn't do it. Sat in the car for like three hours.

(Silence.)

JOSH. I've been sleeping in the tent for about five weeks now. Maybe six.

(Pause.)

MICHAELA. Isn't it starting to get cold at night?

JOSH. Not that bad. And I just sleep down here sometimes.

(Pause.)

MICHAELA. Why?

*(The kettle whistles. **JOSH** unplugs it, opens a cup of ramen noodles.)*

JOSH. You want some?

MICHAELA. No, thanks.

*(**JOSH** throws the top layer of vegetables in the trash. He prepares the noodles.)*

Don't throw away the vegetables! Seriously, that's the only nutritious part. I can't believe you're still eating those things, I was hoping you would outgrow that –

JOSH. You realize that Dad just got worse after you left, right?

(Pause.)

MICHAELA. Yeah, I know –

JOSH. Dad started drinking *more*, as if that was even humanly possible –

MICHAELA. I know –

JOSH. We had *nothing*, when I was in junior high half the time I'd get dinner by going to the Albertson's and eating the free samples, I started working at the car wash when I was sixteen just so we could keep up with the mortgage, I'm *still* working there –

MICHAELA. I know, Josh –

JOSH. When you ran off nine years ago with – what's his name – Brandon?

MICHAELA. Brendan.

JOSH. When you ran off with some stupid drug addict you left me *behind*, with *nothing* –

MICHAELA. What do you want me to say?! I needed to get out of here! I was sixteen and I was stupid, and I needed to get out. If I could have taken you with me, I would have.

JOSH. Oh don't say that, you never would / have –

MICHAELA. You think I went to Eugene because I wanted to *party?* I left because finally – *finally* – there was a way out. And believe me, it wasn't fun. Brendan turned out to be quite the asshole, when I realized he was stealing from me I left him and wound up sleeping in my car for over a year, and – ...

> *(Pause.)*

Running off to Eugene was the biggest mistake of my life, but I am barely, *barely* standing on my own two feet right now. And I'm sorry I didn't come when Dad died, but I spent my last hundred bucks on gas to come out here and keep you from making the biggest mistake of your life.

> *(They stare at each other. Uncomfortable silence.)*
>
> *(Then finally:)*

Also I *really* don't like Ada.

> *(Pause. Then,* **JOSH** *smiles.* **MICHAELA** *smiles as well.)*

JOSH. I know you don't.

MICHAELA. I mean like *really*. And she *hasn't changed.*

JOSH. She's okay.

MICHAELA. She's *insufferable.* She hasn't changed *at all* since high school. Even the haircut, it's so – ...

> *(Pause.)*

JOSH. Your last hundred bucks? I thought you had a job.

MICHAELA. I'm sort of – figuring some stuff out right now.

JOSH. What happened to the – phone surveys, or –?

MICHAELA. Telemarketing.

JOSH. Right.

MICHAELA. I just – ... I couldn't stand it anymore.

> *(Pause.)*

Also, I might have been – let go.

JOSH. What happened?

MICHAELA. It was a couple days after Dad died, and I was just… And this woman on the phone was being *terrible*, she started yelling at me about how I interrupted her "reading hour," as if that was a *thing*, and I – …I screwed up.

JOSH. How?

     (Pause.)

MICHAELA. I called her a fuckface.

     (Pause. **JOSH** *smiles.)*

It's not funny.

JOSH. I'm sorry –

MICHAELA. It's *not funny*.

JOSH. I just haven't heard that in a *while* –

MICHAELA. *Anyway.*

     (Pause.)

When I was at the house today, I realized – there's nothing keeping me in Eugene. And I thought, maybe I could – come back here. For good.

     (Pause. **JOSH** *looks at her.)*

MICHAELA. I could stay with you in the house, find work here in / town –

JOSH. The house is falling apart, Mickey, the bank's about to foreclose on it –

MICHAELA. Well I can get a job, we can keep the house! We can live there together, fix it up. I just think this could be a chance for us to start over. And maybe starting over doesn't have to involve moving to some war zone.

     (Short pause.)

Yeah?

     (Pause.)

JOSH. Wait, so – … So then you're just back for *you*, then.

(**MICHAELA** *looks at him.*)

MICHAELA. What?

JOSH. You lost your job, you don't have any money. It's not about me.

MICHAELA. *No, Josh, I –* … I came back because you're about to make a *huge mistake*, and / you –

JOSH. And my name is on the deed to the house.

(*Short pause.*)

You know actually, I think I'm gonna go for a drive or something.

(**JOSH** *gets up.*)

MICHAELA. Wait – Josh, that is *not* the reason that / I –

JOSH. If you're gonna stay here then just make sure the door locks behind you?

(**JOSH** *starts heading up the stairs.*)

MICHAELA. Do you remember that time Dad locked you out of the house?

(**JOSH** *stops. Pause.*)

Do you?

(*Pause.*)

JOSH. No, I / don't –

MICHAELA. I spent *one night* at Christy Woodburn's house for her birthday sleepover, Dad was so mad that he pulled you out of bed and forced you outside in the snow, in your pajamas, locked the door behind you. The next morning I found you curled up on the porch, wrapped up in a tarp you found in the barn. You were *five years old.* I didn't let you out of my sight for *months* after that. *One night* I spent being a normal girl, and that's how he punished both of us.

(*Short pause.*)

You don't remember any of that?

(*Pause.*)

JOSH. No.

MICHAELA. Thank God.

(Short pause.)

Look – I'm sorry that I wasn't here when he died, but don't you dare act like I'm here for any reason other than to keep you safe.

*(Pause. **JOSH** looks at her for a moment, then descends a couple steps.)*

Can we just – …? Can we please just talk?

*(**JOSH** looks at her.)*

TWO DAYS TO DEPARTURE

Morning.

(The next day. **DENISE** *and* **MARCUS** *sit together, a distance between them.)*

(Silence.)

MARCUS. We could practice more.

(Pause.)

There's those YouTube videos. Like tutorials.

(Pause.)

I just think once you're comfortable praying in tongues you're really gonna like it.

DENISE. Marcus, it's – …

(Pause, gently.)

Honey, I never told you I wasn't comfortable speaking in tongues.

MARCUS. It's just like – sometimes you say the same words over and over?

(Pause.)

Maybe you're overthinking it. The point is *not* to think, you just ask for the spirit and it comes, you don't need to like *think* about the words, they just come. You know?

(Pause.)

And I just think it'd be awesome for you to work on it so it's something we can do as a family. I mean eventually.

*(**DENISE** gets up, looking up the stairs.)*

DENISE. She said noon, right?

MARCUS. The YouTube videos are actually pretty cool.

DENISE. What time is it?

MARCUS. Some of them say that you should start slow, and then maybe work your / way up to speaking more –

DENISE. You know there are different ways to pray, honey.

> *(Pause.)*

MARCUS. What?

DENISE. We talked about this – we don't always have to do things the same way. Sometimes we can do different things, and that doesn't say anything bad about our marriage. Sometimes we can just be different. Do you remember when we talked about that?

> *(Pause.)*

We can watch some videos at home later.

MARCUS. Awesome.

DENISE. I'll get better at it.

MARCUS. That's great babe, I really think you can get better at it.

> *(Pause. **MARCUS** gets up, wrapping his arms around **DENISE**.)*

The next few years are gonna be awesome.

DENISE. I know.

> *(Pause.)*

MARCUS. You know I just want you to be happy, that's all that I want. I just want all of us to be happy.

> *(Pause. **MARCUS** moves his hands down to **DENISE**'s stomach.)*

You, me and this little guy.

DENISE. Or girl.

MARCUS. Guy means both.

> *(**ADA** enters.)*

ADA. Hey guys, sorry about that. Asife, asife! [Sorry, sorry!]

MARCUS. No problem.

ADA. I just wanted to talk with Pastor Chuck about everything, and / he –

DENISE. Wait, he –? You told him?

ADA. Well, of course I told him!

MARCUS. Of course she told him, babe.

ADA. He's super excited for you! Sorry just one sec, I need some water or I'm literally going to die right now.

> (**ADA** *goes to the kitchenette, grabs a cup, and fills it with water.*)
>
> (**DENISE** *looks at* **MARCUS.**)

MARCUS. What?

> (**DENISE** *looks away.*)
>
> (**ADA** *takes a big drink, going back to* **DENISE** *and* **MARCUS.**)

ADA. Okay! So we had a great chat, and I went ahead and called the people from ECL overseas –

DENISE. You told the ECL / people?

ADA. And they're so happy for you! They assured me that you're gonna be *fine* over there, in fact one of the missionaries who's going to be in the capital with us during our whole stay is a doctor from Wisconsin or something, so you'll be totally great.

MARCUS. Awesome.

ADA. And they said as long as your doctor's okay with you flying at six-and-a-half months, then it shouldn't be a problem at all –

DENISE. I just – …

> (*Pause.*)

I'm only two months along. That's early to be / telling people –

MARCUS. Two and a half, babe.

DENISE. Still, it's –. It's still the first trimester, when we told you yesterday, I just thought it was like, between us –

ADA. Oh honey, you're going to be *fine.* And you wanna get everyone praying for you and that kid sooner rather than later, right? So. There's just one other thing, but I actually think you guys are gonna be really excited about it. I was talking yesterday with this guy at the main office, and he was saying – have I mentioned Charlie?

MARCUS. Um…

DENISE. I'm not sure?

ADA. Oh you guys will *love* this guy, he's like this big guy from Boston, and he has that accent, you know? Like – oh, I can't do it. It's like… The – … The front yaaahrd… The front – … Anyway you'll love him, he's sort of like the heart of the organization out there, he's doing all the day-to-day stuff in the mission office in the capital. And we were talking about how he's like, *totally* overwhelmed these days, and now with more people coming over he could really use some help in the office, so – I was thinking that you guys would be a perfect match for that.

MARCUS. Oh yeah?

ADA. Basically it means you'll be doing a little less like on-the-ground witnessing, you'll mostly be working out of the office. And there's even a nice little apartment in the same building that they'll be renting out for you.

MARCUS. That sounds perfect!

ADA. And it's *air-conditioned,* which is gonna be great for you, especially when you start getting *bigger* and –

DENISE. Wait, so – we're not going to be out witnessing?

> *(Pause.)*

ADA. I mean maybe here and there, but you could – …

> *(Pause.)*

I just think maybe you could do something a little more – low impact.

MARCUS. I think this could be *really great.*

DENISE. I – ... I really think we could do a lot of good work out there with the rest of you, we don't have to –

ADA. And I mean also with your guys' nerves about going over there –

DENISE. I'm not nervous.

MARCUS. Denise.

    (Pause.)

ADA. I just thought this could be best for you guys.

MARCUS. This sounds great, Ada. It really does.

    (Pause.)

DENISE. Let's just – ...

    (Pause.)

    Let's not tell anyone else right now?

MARCUS. Babe this is something to *celebrate*, this is –

DENISE. *I'd just rather we don't tell anyone else right now.*

    (Pause.)

ADA. Great!

Afternoon.

(Shortly later. DENISE, ADA, TOM, MARCUS, *and* JOSH.*)*

*(*TOM *is addressing* ADA.*)*

TOM. So you're a Muslim?

ADA. Yes.

TOM. Your family, they're all Muslims?

ADA. Oh yes.

TOM. Have you ever heard of Jesus?

ADA. I think so.

TOM. Mohammed believed that Jesus was a very holy man, did you know that?

ADA. *(Breaking character.)* Okay good, but remember – you want to keep centered on Christ. So maybe something like – Christ actually came before Mohammed, did you know that?

TOM. Okay.

> *(Pause.)*

So Christ actually came before Mohammed, did you know that?

ADA. No. But I'm not white, so I can't be a Christian.

TOM. Actually Christianity doesn't have anything to do with race, or where you were born. Anyone can become a Christian. I'd love to talk with you more about this, do you think you'd like to come to church with me?

ADA. *(Breaking character.)* Okay great!

> *(Everyone applauds.)*

That was great! Mumtez! Maybe it was a *little* quick there, you could spend some more time asking about their home life, getting to know them, you / know –

TOM. Oh yeah, I just didn't know if you like had a full backstory made up or / anything –

ADA. La mooshkele! Don't worry, you don't have to explain, I'm just giving tips!

TOM. Sure.

ADA. Why don't we mix it up again, who wants to go?

(**MARCUS** *stands up.* **TOM** *sits down.*)

MARCUS. *(Awkward joke.)* Okay, who wants to convert me! I'm a heathen!

DENISE. Marcus.

ADA. Josh you want to go?

(**JOSH** *stands up.*)

JOSH. Okay. Hi, my name is Josh.

MARCUS. *(Another awkward joke.)* My name is Allah!

DENISE. *Marcus.*

(*No one laughs. Short pause.*)

MARCUS. I'm Saeed.

JOSH. Hi, Saeed. Do you live here in the village?

MARCUS. Yeah, totally. Been here my entire life.

JOSH. That's great. So you must have grown up in a Muslim household?

MARCUS. Oh yeah. They're all Muslims.

JOSH. And you went to a Muslim school?

MARCUS. Yep.

JOSH. What was the name of the school?

(*Pause.*)

MARCUS. What?

ADA. This is good! He's asking personal details, this is good. Keep going.

(*Pause.*)

MARCUS. Okay, it's called – Koran School. I don't know?

JOSH. Do all of your siblings go there too?

MARCUS. Uh yeah, probably.

JOSH. What are their names?

MARCUS. *(Totally dropping character.)* Josh, c'mon.

ADA. No, this is good!

*(*MARCUS *looks at* ADA.*)*

MARCUS. I don't know, like, names.

ADA. That's okay!

(Pause. MARCUS *glares at* JOSH.*)*

MARCUS. I just have one brother, his name is – Mohammed, I guess.

JOSH. That's great. So what are your parents' names?

*(*TOM *giggles.*)*

MARCUS. *(To* ADA.*)* Okay he's just making fun of me now.

ADA. Josh let's just say you've gotten to know him a little bit, now let's bring it around.

JOSH. Okay.

(To MARCUS.*)*

So, I'm a Christian. Have you ever met any Christians?

MARCUS. Yeah, maybe. Not really. No.

JOSH. I know that you probably don't know very much about Christ and his message, but I can tell you – it really helped me.

MARCUS. Oh yeah?

JOSH. Yeah. There was a point in my life, when I was younger, when things were really bad for me –

ADA. Good! This is great, keep going.

JOSH. – But my relationship with Jesus really helped me, it really –

ADA. Get personal with him!

(Pause.)

JOSH. *(To* ADA.*)* You want me to –?

ADA. Open up! Personal testimony about being born again is always effective.

JOSH. Okay, well – …

(To MARCUS.*)*

I was – young. Twelve, thirteen. And things in my life were pretty bad, my family was – … And I didn't really know what my future was, I didn't really have a reason to get out of bed in the morning. But then my best friend from school invited me to go to church with him.

(**JOSH** *looks at* **TOM**.)

ADA. Aw.

JOSH. And my life was changed forever. I had a reason to get out of bed in the morning. I know why – …

(*Pause.*)

I guess – I know why I'm alive.

(*Pause.*)

ADA. Josh – that was *powerful.*

(**ADA** *starts clapping.* **TOM**, **DENISE**, *and* **MARCUS** *join in.*)

JOSH. Thanks.

ADA. Does someone want to go in for Josh?

(*No one volunteers.*)

Denise, why don't you go?

DENISE. Oh, sure.

(**JOSH** *sits down*, **DENISE** *stands up.*)

ADA. Why don't you guys flip it? Marcus, why don't you witness to Denise?

DENISE. So I get to like make up a character?

ADA. Yeah sure.

DENISE. Great, I'm actually good at this I think.

ADA. Okay great. Go for it!

(*Pause.* **MARCUS** *looks at* **DENISE**.)

MARCUS. Hi there.

DENISE. Hello.

(**DENISE** *mimes a basket in her hands.*)

Would you like to buy some eggs?

(*Pause.*)

MARCUS. What?

DENISE. I help my family by selling eggs on the street. Would you like to buy some eggs from me?

ADA. Nice!

(*Short pause.*)

MARCUS. Oh, uh – sure, I'll take an egg.

DENISE. We live on a farm outside of the village, but five years ago my father was killed in the uprising. So my brother and I had to leave school and start earning money to support our mother. She has been quite sick ever since our well was contaminated. So now we sell our white and brown eggs on the streets. How interesting! The white eggs match your pale skin while the brown eggs fit my darker complexion!

ADA. Okay, let's – … Denise that was super creative, but – maybe try something more – simple?

DENISE. Oh.

ADA. I mean that was great but this is more of an exercise for Marcus, you know

DENISE. (*Crestfallen.*) Okay.

(*Pause, to* MARCUS.*)*

Hello.

MARCUS. Hi there. My name is Marcus. I came here with my wife Denise, all the way from America.

DENISE. Great.

MARCUS. And I'd really like the opportunity to talk to you more about Jesus. Would you like to come to church with me, meet some of my friends?

(*Pause.*)

DENISE. Okay.

(*Pause.* DENISE *looks at* ADA*, starts clapping tepidly.* TOM *and* JOSH *awkwardly join in.*)

ADA. Okay good yeah, just –. You can make it hard for him.

DENISE. Really?

ADA. Yeah! That's what this is all about. Make it tough for him!

DENISE. Oh, okay.

(Pause.)

Hi there.

MARCUS. Hi. My name is Marcus. I came here from America so I can tell people all about Jesus. Do you know anything about Jesus?

DENISE. Yes, a little.

MARCUS. Are you a Muslim?

DENISE. I grew up Muslim, but now I don't believe in God.

ADA. Interesting! Okay keep going.

(Pause.)

MARCUS. Do you mind if I ask why you don't believe in God?

DENISE. I just think that it's torn my country apart. People believing different things about God, and arguing about those differences.

MARCUS. Truth, truth. People in your country have been arguing about different versions of Islam for forever, but – the thing is, you can choose a different path. My faith in Christ doesn't put me in harm's way – it keeps me safe.

ADA. Oh gosh, Marcus, that was / really –

DENISE. I disagree.

(Pause. MARCUS turns to DENISE.)

MARCUS. What?

DENISE. Christianity has killed many people as well, it continues to kill people all around the world. You just live in America, and in America right now it's safe to be a Christian, but that doesn't mean that it was always like that, or it'll still be like that in the future.

ADA. Okay, this is good – Marcus, take it out of the realm of politics, point out that faith is bigger than politics, this is about their personal relationship with Jesus –

MARCUS. Right, it's about your personal relationship with Jesus, it's / about –

DENISE. For me this is superstition. I think that basically you are only Christian because your parents are Christian, and in general people are only religious because they fear death.

TOM. Woah.

ADA. Okay, this is good, keep going.

(MARCUS *looks at* DENISE, *puzzled.*)

MARCUS. Okay, I –. I'm not afraid of death, I just – …

ADA. Okay use the pop can argument, remember? The one that Pastor Chuck gave us, the –?

MARCUS. Oh right! Okay, so. So if there is no God, then we're like – … Crap, I can't –. Ada, I can't / remember –

ADA. We're all just chemical reactions, there's no meaning to it, we're just like pop cans that get shaken up when we're born and we just fizz for a while until we stop, there's no / point to it –

DENISE. Maybe! Maybe we are just cans of pop fizzing, maybe our lives have a beginning and an end, and maybe we just need to be okay with that. Maybe we waste so much time worrying about what will happen to us after we die that we don't make meaning out of the lives we are given. Maybe – we should all just grow up and be okay with living a life.

(*Silence. Everyone looks at* DENISE.)

Are we – …?

(*Pause.*)

Are we still going?

Night.

(Much later. **JOSH** *sits alone at the piano, staring at it. After a moment, he lifts up the key cover and puts his hands on the keyboard.)*

(Slowly, he begins to play the second movement of Beethoven's "Appassionata.")

*(***TOM*** *comes down the stairs. He watches* **JOSH** *as he continues to play.)*

(Just as **JOSH** *is about to finish the phrase at the end of the eighth bar, he stops before playing the final D-flat, lifting his hands off the piano. He looks at the keyboard.)*

(Pause.)

TOM. Why'd you stop?

(Pause.)

JOSH. I –.

(Short pause.)

I don't remember it.

TOM. Yes you do, you've played that for me a thousand times, / you –

JOSH. I don't remember it, I – …

*(***JOSH*** *closes the lid on the keyboard.)*

(Silence.)

You have work today?

TOM. Just got off. I drove to your place after, Michaela said you were here.

(Pause. **TOM** *moves to* **JOSH**.*)*

TOM. She wants to move back?

(Pause.)

JOSH. Yeah. She wants us to keep the house, live there together.

TOM. That sounds – really nice.

JOSH. Something's wrong with the foundation, I don't know where we'd get the money to fix that. Needs a new roof in the next few years, too, and –

TOM. So you're thinking about it?

(*Pause.* **JOSH** *looks at* **TOM.**)

JOSH. No, Tom, I'm not.

(*Pause.* **TOM**'s *phone buzzes. He pulls it out of his pocket, looks at it.*)

That your dad?

TOM. Yeah. He's been texting all night.

JOSH. Is something wrong?

TOM. No, he just –.

(*Pause.*)

We just kinda got into this argument, I don't know.

JOSH. About what?

TOM. I just –. It's this constant thing where he asks me to tell him what I'm feeling, and then when I actually tell him the truth, he gets mad, and – …I don't know.

JOSH. What did he say?

(*Pause.*)

TOM. He told me that – he's worried my heart is darkening. That I'm losing my faith.

(*Pause.*)

JOSH. Oh.

TOM. Yeah. It was bad.

(*Pause.*)

(**TOM**'s *phone buzzes again, he looks at it, puts it back in his pocket. He sits with* **JOSH**, *staring forward.*)

When I was driving just now, I was listening to this piece, I don't remember the name of the composer, I hadn't heard of him, but the piece is called "The Quartet for the End of Time." You heard of it?

JOSH. I don't think so?

TOM. It sort of came up randomly when I was looking for music earlier, I started listening to it, and at first I was like – this is *not* my thing, it's too weird, dissonant – but then I kept listening as I was driving and something about it… The whole piece was inspired by this passage from Revelation, the part where – …

(Silence. **TOM** *looks down.)*

JOSH. Tom –

TOM. I don't feel good.

JOSH. What is it?

TOM. I'm just –. I'm nauseous. Pins and needles in my hands.

(JOSH *goes to him.)*

JOSH. Okay –

TOM. I don't feel good –

JOSH. Why don't we pray together?

TOM. Josh –

JOSH. Just pray with me, you'll feel better, just –

TOM. *I don't want to pray right now, Josh, I – …*

(Pause. Finally, **TOM** *takes out his phone and a pair of earbuds.)*

Here.

JOSH. What?

TOM. The quartet, the –. What I was listening to earlier, let's listen to it.

JOSH. Wait, you –? Are you okay?

TOM. I'm fine, just –.

*(***TOM** *scrolls through his phone.)*

JOSH. I really think if you just pray with me, you'll feel better, you'll –

TOM. *(Firmly.)* We don't have a lot of time left. Can't we at least do this? Please?

(Silence. **JOSH** *and* **TOM** *look at one another.)*

JOSH. Okay.

*(***TOM*** scrolls through his phone a bit, lands on something. He gives* **JOSH** *one earbud, putting the other in his ear.)*

TOM. Here, this is my favorite movement.

*(***JOSH*** puts the earbud in his ear.* **TOM** *presses play.)*

(They both listen for seven seconds. They both sit facing out, neither of them looking at one another.)

The cello, it's just so…

(Four seconds. They listen.)

Those big long phrases, they're like – …

*(***JOSH*** looks up. Six more seconds.)*

And the piano comes in… Here.

*(***JOSH*** looks up, his eyes widening.)*

This composer – he was sent to a prison by the Nazis in World War II, and he didn't have a lot of access to instruments other than like this old clarinet and a piano and a cello and – something else? Violin? And he wrote this piece for those instruments, and they performed it outside, in the rain, for all the guards and prisoners. And I started really thinking about it – thinking about being in a place like that, and writing this music…

(Pause.)

Some people have this ability to take their own suffering and turn it into – the opposite of suffering. How do. people do that?

*(***JOSH*** starts to become upset.)*

And it's all inspired by this passage from Revelation, the part where the giant angel comes down, with a face like the sun and legs like pillars of fire – and he declares that time no longer exists.

(Pause.)

Just like that.

(**JOSH** *looks at* **TOM**. *Pause.*)

Time won't exist.

(**JOSH** *suddenly stands up, knocking the phone out of* **TOM**'s *hand. He moves away from* **TOM**, *not looking at him.* **TOM** *picks up the phone, stops the music.*)

(Pause.)

Are you –?

JOSH. Yeah, I'm – …

(**JOSH** *looks at* **TOM**. *A very, very long silence.*)

Tom, I – …

(**JOSH** *stops himself, looks away. Pause.*)

I have a headache.

(Pause.)

TOM. Do you want something?

JOSH. No, it's –.

TOM. You want a pop?

(Pause. **TOM** *goes to the fridge, takes out a can of soda. He brings it to* **JOSH**, *hands it to him.*)

JOSH. Thank you.

(**JOSH** *opens the can, drinks.*)

(Pause. **JOSH** *looks at* **TOM**.*)

We'll Skype, Tom. We'll Skype, we'll keep in touch, it's –.

(Pause.)

We're going to be fine. Both of us. Right?

(They look at one another.)

(Finally, **TOM** *turns away and exits up the stairs.)*

(**JOSH** *stares forward, motionless.*)

ONE DAY TO DEPARTURE

Morning.

(DENISE *sits, pensive. Upstairs we hear the choir repeatedly rehearsing the second verse of "Pass Me Not, O Gentle Savior," in an uncomfortably high key.*)

(MARCUS *enters, descending a few steps. He sees* DENISE. DENISE *looks up, seeing him. She gets up, busies herself with her backpack.*)

(MARCUS *continues down the stairs.*)

MARCUS. What are you [looking for] – ...?

DENISE. Chapstick.

MARCUS. I got some, babe.

DENISE. I don't like yours.

> (DENISE *continues rooting around in her backpack.*)

> (MARCUS *sits down, keeping his distance. A silence.*)

MARCUS. Where did you sleep?

DENISE. Air mattress in my sister's room.

MARCUS. Oh, cool.

> (Pause.)

Do you think you might come home tonight?

> (Pause. DENISE *looks at him for a moment, then goes back to her backpack. She finds her chapstick, then stands up, applying the chapstick to her lips.*)

MARCUS. You're still mad at me.

DENISE. Marcus.

MARCUS. I just think it's gonna be better for us. And it'll be more comfortable, we won't be out all day driving around to little villages, we'll be inside, we'll be safer, and –

DENISE. When did you and Ada meet with Pastor Chuck?

(Pause.)

MARCUS. It was just like – ... It was like a week ago. Maybe two.

DENISE. Why didn't you tell me?

(Pause.)

MARCUS. I just thought – ... I knew you wouldn't like it.

DENISE. You didn't think you should *ask* me first?

MARCUS. I knew you'd say no.

(Pause.)

Look, babe, I'm sorry but I'm just *worried* about you, you know? I wanted to be sure that we could still go over there, that I wouldn't have to worry about you –

DENISE. I told you that I'd be *fine* –

MARCUS. It's Chuck, if we can't tell him then who can we tell?

(Pause.)

I just want you to be safe, babe. Both of you.

(Pause.)

DENISE. Marcus, was it your idea for us to spend all four months working in the mission office?

MARCUS. No.

(Pause.)

Sort of.

(Pause.)

We'll still have fun. And it'll be safer.

DENISE. And you'll be a lot less anxious.

MARCUS. This is about *you*, babe. You and our little guy.

DENISE. *Or. Girl.*

MARCUS. Or girl, or girl.

>   *(Pause.)*
>
>   What did you, uh. I mean what did you tell your parents?

DENISE. About what?

MARCUS. Like – why you're staying with them. Why you're not staying – with me.

>   *(Pause.)*
>
>   I just don't want people to be like up in our business.

>   **(DENISE** *stares at him icily.)*
>
>   **(JOSH** *enters.* **MARCUS** *and* **DENISE** *look away from each other.)*

JOSH. Oh, sorry –

MARCUS. / It's fine.

DENISE. Nothing.

>   **(JOSH** *senses the tension.)*

JOSH. O – kay.

>   *(Pause.* **DENISE** *and* **MARCUS** *look at each other.* **JOSH** *awkwardly starts to go back upstairs.)*

DENISE. You know Josh, if I haven't told you this yet, I just want you to know that I think what you're doing is just really remarkable.

JOSH. Oh.

DENISE. I mean the way that you're just moving out there, I think it's just – beautiful. I think it might be the most inspiring thing I've ever heard of.

>   *(Pause.)*

MARCUS. Yeah, totally.

>   *(Awkward pause. The choir continues.)*

JOSH. Thanks, guys, that's really –

DENISE. I mean you're just *doing it.*

>   *(Pause.)*

JOSH. Yeah.

DENISE. No fear. No fear whatsoever. Just *doing it.*

>   (**DENISE** *looks at* **MARCUS.** *Pause.* **JOSH** *is perplexed.*)

We're actually just going to be working in the office the whole time.

JOSH. Oh.

DENISE. Yeah, we're both just a little nervous about the whole thing, I guess. We're both just so nervous.

>   *(Pause.)*

JOSH. Yeah, well, I get it, it's a big step to –

DENISE. So we're going to spend four months in an office.

>   *(Pause.)*

Because we're both just so nervous.

MARCUS. Babe.

>   *(Awkward silence.)*

>   *(Finally,* **ADA** *enters carrying a Tupperware container.)*

ADA. I made cupcakes!

>   *(Pause.)*

Everything okay?

MARCUS. Yeah we're great.

>   (**ADA** *comes down the stairs into the room. The choir moves on to practicing the refrain [“Savior, savior, hear my humble cry…”], straining to hit even higher notes than before.*)

ADA. Hm. Sandy said she'd be done by ten, that's –. Anyway.

>   *(To the group.)*

I thought we could just have a little party today, I bet we're all a little trained out! Just fellowship today, maybe a little praying?

*(***TOM*** *comes down the stairs.)*

There he is!

TOM. Sorry.

ADA. I made cupcakes!

> *(***ADA*** *opens the Tupperware containers, takes out the cupcakes.)*
>
> *(***TOM*** *comes down the stairs, not looking at* ***JOSH***. ***MARCUS*** *reaches for* ***DENISE***, ***DENISE*** *moves away from him.)*

MARCUS. Babe.

JOSH. *(To* ***TOM***.*)* You okay?

TOM. I'm not – ... I don't feel very –

ADA. No one wants a cupcake?

> *(Pause. No one moves.)*

We're a nervous bunch today!

> *(No one moves.)*

I can't believe that no one wants a cupcake.

> *(Pause, then surprisingly stern.)*

Guys have a cupcake.

> *(Everyone awkwardly moves to the Tupperware container, takes a cupcake.)*
>
> *(***MARCUS***, ***TOM***, ***DENISE***, and ***JOSH*** all find separate areas of the room to stand in.* ***ADA*** *looks at everyone.)*

Now I know that this is a big trip, I know it. But I promise you, you're gonna feel *so much better* when you're actually over there. I promise.

> *(No response. Pause.)*

Okay. Let's bring it in.

> *(***ADA*** *sits on the floor. Everyone awkwardly joins her.)*
>
> *(The choir continues upstairs, repeating the refrain over and over.)*

ADA. Have I ever told you guys about the day I first went over there?

MARCUS. No.

ADA. Well *let me tell you*, you think you guys are nervous? You should have seen me. And I was traveling over there *alone* so you can only imagine. Pastor Chuck was driving me to the airport in Boise, and it was like super rainy for some reason which was *not helping*, and I was looking out the window, and I look up into the sky, and I see – a little rainbow. It just showed up, right then. And that rainbow ended *right. At. The airport.*

DENISE. Rainbows don't end.

(Pause. Everyone looks at DENISE.)

ADA. Hm?

DENISE. It's an optical illusion, they don't actually end anywhere, it just depends on where you're seeing it from.

(Pause.)

I'm just saying it didn't end at the airport, not really.

MARCUS. Babe.

(The choir continues. Another awkward pause.)

ADA. Okay! Well I think we're all wound pretty tight today, so maybe just a cupcake and some prayer, and then we all go home to get a good night's rest –

*(**TOM** suddenly vomits on the floor.)*

/ Oh. Oh, my –

MARCUS. / Woah –

JOSH. Tom –

*(**ADA** goes to **TOM**, unsure of what to do.)*

ADA. Okay, uh. Why don't you just take a breath, and – …

(Trying to make light of it.)

Wow, someone really is nervous, isn't he! Marcus, could you –?

(**ADA** *goes to get* **TOM** *some water.* **MARCUS** *grabs
some paper towels, starts cleaning up the vomit.*)

MARCUS. Buddy, you getting nervous about the trip?

TOM. No –

ADA. It's *completely fine to be nervous* –

. (**JOSH** *goes to* **TOM**, *putting his hand on* **TOM**'s
back.*)

JOSH. Tom, it's okay –

TOM. Stop.

(**JOSH** *gets closer to* **TOM**, *putting both of his
hands on* **TOM**'s *shoulders, trying to comfort him.*)

ADA. Okay, Tom, let's just take a breath –

TOM. (*Losing himself, pushing* **JOSH** *away.*) *Stop touching me, I
don't want you to take care of me! Just leave me alone, I –* …

(*Silence.* **TOM** *and* **JOSH** *stare at one another.*)

(**TOM** *quickly exits, heading upstairs.*)

(*A tense silence.*)

ADA. Okay, could everyone just –? I think that's it for today.

(*Everyone disperses.* **MARCUS** *and* **DENISE** *head
upstairs.* **JOSH** *stands up.*)

Hang back for a minute, Josh?

(**JOSH** *looks at* **ADA**.*)

(*Upstairs, the choir finally finishes.*)

(**DENISE** *and* **MARCUS** *are gone.* **ADA** *looks at*
JOSH.*)

(*Silence.*)

So!

(*Pause.*)

What's up?

(*Pause.*)

JOSH. Tom didn't – … He's just been – upset lately.

ADA. Oh, sure. He's – a sensitive guy. This has to be really hard for you.

> *(Pause.)*

And having your sister come back to town, that's gotta be...

> *(Pause.)*

Tom and Michaela don't want you to move over there, do they?

> (**JOSH** *looks at her.*)

It's okay!

JOSH. No, they –. They don't.

> *(Pause.)*

Michaela's talking about moving back to town.

ADA. Well that could be really good for her!

> *(Pause.)*

Now I just want to make sure this doesn't have any impact on your plans, or –

JOSH. No, of course not, I'm going.

ADA. Well that's good!

> *(Pause.)*

Because you know we already paid for your ticket, and ECL is expecting you, it would look pretty bad for the whole church if you –

JOSH. I'm going. Of course I'm going.

> (**ADA** *smiles at him, then turns toward her cupcakes.*)

ADA. I spent two hours this morning making these. Should have been doing my Arabic flashcards instead, I guess. Did you even get to taste one?

JOSH. Oh, I – ...

> (**JOSH** *goes to his cupcake on the ground, picking it up. He goes to the kitchenette, throws it away,*

then grabs some paper towels. **ADA** *and* **JOSH**
throw away the remaining cupcakes.)

ADA. You wanna split the last one with me? I put real lemon
zest in the frosting.

    *(***ADA** *splits a cupcake, hands one half to* **JOSH**.
    JOSH *sits down with his cupcake. They eat.)*

You know, I can't tell you how much I admire you for
what you're doing. Pastor Chuck, too.

JOSH. Yeah, I – ...

    (Pause.)

I guess I just want – something to happen.

ADA. What do you mean?

JOSH. I mean like these stories that you tell – the rainbow
showing up, right when you needed it, the prostitute
that you met on the street when you were over there? I
guess I just feel like – that's what I'm waiting for. Some,
like, little signal or whatever, something to let me know
that I'm on the right path, that this is what I need to
spend the rest of my life doing.

    (Pause. **ADA** *puts her cupcake down.)*

ADA. Josh you're a really smart guy.

    (Pause. **JOSH** *looks at her.)*

JOSH. Thank you.

ADA. I mean, I'm just saying – you're a smart guy. I'm a
smart gal, you're a smart guy.

    (Pause.)

JOSH. I don't really know what / you –

ADA. I remember when I was like ten or eleven, I was
traveling with my parents down in Brazil? We were
just like going to different churches, meeting people,
handing out tracts. I mean it was mostly a vacation,
most of the time we were at this resort dealie, but we
also did some witnessing. Anyways we were at this one
church and this Brazilian pastor was telling his story,

he told everyone about how when he was younger he had a lot of hatred toward Christianity, he even used to steal money from his family's church. And this one night he was walking through an alley, and he sees this blinding light and a guy appears in front of him and says, "My name is Jesus. Why are you persecuting me?" And I remember I was thinking – this is like, *really* similar to Paul's conversion story from Acts, right? Like *really* similar.

JOSH. Yeah.

ADA. And I almost said something to my dad, but then I looked around and everyone in the crowd was *super* moved. And you could tell, this guy was *full* of the spirit. The spirit was more important than whether or not it like, *actually* happened *exactly* that way.

> *(Pause.* **ADA** *picks her cupcake back up, starts picking at it.)*

JOSH. Wait, what do you mean?

ADA. I just mean – you're a smart guy! You're smart enough to know that faith is enough by itself, you don't need the magic tricks. Faith and the spirit, that's always enough.

> *(Pause.)*

JOSH. Wait, so – are you saying that the stories you tell, they aren't true?

ADA. No! They're true!

> *(**ADA** licks some frosting off her finger.)*

Mm, cream cheese frosting. Seriously, if you put cream cheese frosting on a stapler, I would eat that stapler.   ·

> *(Pause.)*

And you know Michaela hasn't like, totally proven that she's always going to be there for you. Just saying.

> *(Pause.)*

So are you all packed?

> *(Pause.* **JOSH** *looks at her.)*

Darkness.

(As the lights go to black, we begin to hear the sound of rain, light at first, then growing in intensity.)

(The sound builds until the theater is surrounded by the sound of pouring rain, growing in volume, until lights rise on:)

Night.

(The sound of pelting rain outside. The lights are all off except for the lamp on the piano. **TOM** *and* **MICHAELA** *sit together.)*

*(***TOM*** *has his phone to his ear. Pause.)*

MICHAELA. Nothing?

(Pause. **TOM** *lowers the phone.)*

TOM. Just voicemail.

(Pause.)

I'm sure he's fine.

MICHAELA. His bag is here, he / has to –

TOM. I don't know, I haven't –. I haven't seen him.

(Short pause.)

He's not going to listen to you.

MICHAELA. He might listen to you.

(Pause.)

I'm out of ideas. I haven't heard from him all day, you guys are on a plane in less than twelve hours, I have to do *something*.

*(***TOM*** *looks away. Pause.)*

TOM. Look I have to go, I haven't finished packing for tomorrow and –

MICHAELA. I just don't – …

TOM. What?

MICHAELA. I'm sorry, I *just don't understand all this shit.* All these years, I knew he was going to a church, but I didn't…

(Pause.)

Can you please just help me understand what's going on with him?

(Pause.)

TOM. I don't know. Those few days after your dad died, he barely even *talked*. If I didn't bring him food I don't think he would have eaten anything at all. And the only thing your dad left him was debt, so he had to keep working which was awful for him.

> *(Pause.)*

MICHAELA. But he – he took care of the burial and everything, he –?

TOM. I took up a collection at the church, handled it all myself.

MICHAELA. Oh.

> *(Pause.)*

Thank you.

> *(Pause.)*

> *(***TOM****'s phone buzzes, he looks at it.)*

TOM. It's my dad, I –. I really have to go –

MICHAELA. Do you – …?

> *(Pause.)*

TOM. What?

MICHAELA. It's just that you seem – smart.

TOM. Yeah?

MICHAELA. And you really believe in all this stuff? You really believe you're going on some crusade to save souls?

> *(Pause.)*

TOM. You think I'm simple.

MICHAELA. No –

TOM. You do, but it's okay.

> *(Pause.)*

You know, it's not like we're all *unaware* of how secular people view us. We know that you think we're silly, superstitious, backward.

MICHAELA. I didn't say that.

TOM. But you're thinking it.

(Pause.)

TOM. I'm not going to pretend to know everything about theology, I'm still figuring stuff out. But, I guess, when it comes down to it – when given the choice between a world governed by absolutes, a world in which there is immutable right and immutable wrong – I choose that world. Given the choice between believing that I'm going to see my mother again someday, and believing that she's just a pile of ash sitting in a jar somewhere, I – ...

(Pause. TOM shrugs, looks away.)

MICHAELA. Yeah.

(JOSH enters, completely soaked. TOM and MICHAELA look at him. Pause.)

MICHAELA. God, Josh, what –? What are you doing?

JOSH. I was just – ... I was just walking.

MICHAELA. In the middle of a storm?

(JOSH descends a few steps, looks at TOM.)

I was worried, I was calling your phone over and over –

JOSH. Oh, I –. I left it in my backpack, I think. I don't know.

(Pause. JOSH goes to the kitchenette, taking a cup of ramen noodles. He takes off the packaging.)

MICHAELA. *(To TOM.)* Is there a towel, or –?

(TOM starts rooting around in the kitchenette.)

JOSH. I'm fine.

MICHAELA. You're soaked.

JOSH. It's just water.

MICHAELA. How long were you out there?

JOSH. I – don't know, I guess.

(TOM pulls out a large tablecloth, hands it to JOSH.)

TOM. There aren't any towels.

JOSH. That's fine.

(**JOSH** *wraps the tablecloth around his shoulders.*)

I've never seen rain like that here, that like – *constant* downpour. I kept expecting it to stop, but it just kept coming. After I was out there for an hour or two, I was like – it has to end, the rain has to let up eventually. But it just kept coming.

MICHAELA. Why were you out walking in the rain?

JOSH. I don't know, I – ...

(*Pause.*)

I guess I just realized I wanted to walk around town a bit. Realized that maybe it was my last chance.

(*Pause.*)

When I was walking I had this weird thought, like I was imagining all that rain hitting the fields, and I was picturing the fields back at the farm, thinking about the crop coming back. And I felt so – ...

(*Pause.*)

Did I boil water? I can't remember if I boiled water.

(**JOSH** *starts to move toward the kitchenette,* **MICHAELA** *blocks him.*)

MICHAELA. Get in my car.

JOSH. What?

MICHAELA. Go upstairs and get into my car, right now.

JOSH. Why?

MICHAELA. We're going home. Enough of this bullshit, enough of this basement, enough of the weird half-answers, you're going home with me – *now* – and we're going to talk. For real.

JOSH. I'm making food.

(**JOSH** *tries to go to the kitchenette,* **MICHAELA** *continues to block him.*)

MICHAELA. Get upstairs.

TOM. Michaela –

JOSH. You can't tell me what to do, Mickey.

MICHAELA. The hell I can't, get upstairs, *now*.

> (**JOSH** *laughs.*)

JOSH. I'll see you tomorrow morning before I leave, Mickey, I –

> (**JOSH** *again tries to go to the kitchenette.* **MICHAELA** *grabs the kettle, moving away from* **JOSH.**)

TOM. Okay, / guys –

JOSH. Gimme that.

MICHAELA. Make me.

TOM. *Guys.*

> (**JOSH** *wrestles the kettle away from* **MICHAELA.**)

JOSH. *Stop it.*

MICHAELA. Get in my car, *now*.

JOSH. You're not in charge of me, you / don't get to –

MICHAELA. Do you even know what it's going to be like over there?! Do you know how *dangerous* it is over there, right now?

JOSH. Yes, I do, / I –

MICHAELA. You think everyone over there is gonna sit down with you and drink tea and talk about *Jesus*? I looked on the website, Josh, I read about it, I didn't see too much about helping people, it was just about *converting* them –

JOSH. You're the most selfish person I've ever known, you know that?

MICHAELA. Okay, here we go.

JOSH. What would you know about helping people?

MICHAELA. I practically *raised you* –

JOSH. And you hated every second of it! You couldn't go two days without reminding me what a burden I was, / how you didn't have a life because of me –

MICHAELA. Mom left when I was *seven years old*, do you think I wanted to be stuck with changing your / shitty diapers?

TOM. Guys, / *please*, just calm down –

JOSH. And you just *run away*, you *leave me behind* –

MICHAELA. I needed to save myself!

JOSH. *What about me?!*

MICHAELA. I'm saving you *now*!

JOSH. Yeah well you're too late for that –

MICHAELA. What if you get sick over there, what if something happens?

JOSH. There are doctors, there are hospitals –

MICHAELA. What if you get *shot*, Josh?! Did you think about that?! You could *die over there* –

JOSH. *(Exploding.)* AND THAT WOULD BE A MIRACLE. THAT WOULD BE A *FUCKING MIRACLE*.

> *(Silence.)*

> *(JOSH breathes. MICHAELA and TOM watch him.)*

> *(Finally, JOSH moves to the kitchenette, about to plug in the electric kettle. He stops, drops the cord on the counter.)*

> *(Silence.)*

I saw it coming about a week before it actually happened. Maybe a little more than that.

> *(Pause.)*

His eyes had been this bright yellow, this like – electric yellow. Skin was getting pretty yellow, too. He hadn't said a word to me for weeks, maybe even months. I moved into the tent outside because I couldn't watch it happen anymore. He'd stand in the big windows over the kitchen sink and watch me as I boiled water on the camping stove or heated up Chef Boyardee, or –. Forty acres of barley rotting behind me, and this man – always in this window – getting smaller, smaller…

(Pause.)

JOSH. In the middle of the night he came to me. I heard the zipper on my tent open and I woke up, he was standing over me, and he bent down and looked at me with those bright yellow eyes and said: "You need to know – that there is no God." And I didn't say anything. Then he just turned around, went back inside. And two days later I found him face down on the kitchen floor and my first thought was – wow, that was the last thing that he ever said to me.

(Pause.)

But I knew if I made this decision, if I said that I was going to commit the *rest* of my *life* to serving God, then He would have to show up in my life. He would. JUST SHOW UP. SHOW UP. *SHOW UP.*

*(*JOSH *slumps down to the floor,* MICHAELA *catches him. They both go down to the floor.* TOM *watches, unsure of what to do.)*

MICHAELA. It's okay –

JOSH. I can't go back to the house –

MICHAELA. It's okay –

JOSH. I can't go back there, Mickey, I really can't...

(Short pause.)

MICHAELA. Then let's just go.

(Pause. JOSH *looks at* MICHAELA. MICHAELA *sits on the floor facing him.)*

JOSH. What do you mean?

MICHAELA. Let's just get out of here. Leave town.

(Pause.)

JOSH. Mickey, I don't – ...

(Pause.)

I can't –

MICHAELA. Why not?

JOSH. I can't just –, they bought me a plane ticket, they have everything set up, I can't – …

> *(Pause.)*

I can't tell them I'm not going.

MICHAELA. So don't tell them. Just come with me.

> *(Pause.)*

> *(***JOSH*** looks at* **TOM**.*)*

JOSH. Mickey I don't know –

MICHAELA. You don't have to tell them anything, let's just go.

> *(Pause.)*

Okay?

> *(***JOSH*** looks at* **MICHAELA**. *Pause.)*

JOSH. Okay.

MICHAELA. Okay. *Thank God –*

JOSH. If I call you.

> *(Pause.)*

MICHAELA. What?

JOSH. If I call you tomorrow morning – then we go together.

> *(Silence.)*

MICHAELA. Okay. If you call me.

> *(Pause.* **MICHAELA** *gets up.)*

MICHAELA. I'll be ready, okay? The car'll be packed, I'll be ready to go.

JOSH. Okay.

MICHAELA. And you *call me tomorrow.* Okay?

> *(***JOSH*** looks at her.* **MICHAELA** *looks at* **TOM**, *then exits up the stairs.)*

> *(***JOSH*** stays on the ground.)*

> *(***TOM*** sits down on the ground, keeping his distance from* **JOSH**.*)*

(Silence.)

TOM. Are you gonna go with her?

(Pause.)

JOSH. I don't know. I don't know if I have it in me.

*(Silence. **TOM**'s phone starts buzzing. He takes it out of his pocket, looking at it. It continues to buzz.)*

*(**TOM** silences the phone, puts it on the floor. Pause.)*

(Finally:)

TOM. I could go with you.

*(Pause. **JOSH** looks at **TOM**.)*

If you go with your sister, I could come too.

(Pause.)

JOSH. Tom –

TOM. I'll do it, seriously.

JOSH. You can't say that to me unless you really mean it –

TOM. I mean it. I do.

(Pause.)

It terrifies me too, but – I mean we can figure it out, right?

*(Pause. **JOSH** looks at **TOM**, then looks to the ground.)*

JOSH. God, I don't know. God.

*(**JOSH** slowly lays down on the ground, still wrapped in the tablecloth. He closes his eyes.)*

*(Pause. **TOM** goes to him, lying next to him. After a moment he wraps his arms around **JOSH**.)*

(They both breathe, lying on the floor together.)

(A long silence, the only sound is the rain coming from upstairs.)

I guess, I just – don't know why I'm alive.

(Pause.)

I wish I knew why I'm alive.

(Pause.)

TOM. I don't know.

(Pause.)

We'll try to figure it out.

(Pause.)

We have time.

(Pause.)

JOSH. Yeah.

DEPARTURE DAY

Dawn.

(**TOM** *and* **JOSH** *are lying on the floor, asleep, in the same positions as they were in at the end of the last scene, wrapped in each other's arms. The lights are all off.*)

(*After a moment, we hear someone descending the stairs. Slowly,* **CHUCK** *emerges. He descends a few steps, sees* **TOM** *and* **JOSH** *lying on the floor together. He looks at them for a brief moment, then continues down the stairs.*)

(*He goes to* **TOM** *and* **JOSH**, *standing over them, studying them.*)

CHUCK. (*Simply.*) Hm.

(*Pause.* **CHUCK** *slowly goes to the light switch, flipping it.*)

(**TOM** *slowly opens his eyes, lifting his head. He sees* **CHUCK** *on the other side of the room.*)

(*He darts away from* **JOSH** *as quickly as he can into a corner, sitting on the ground, staring at* **CHUCK**.)

(**JOSH** *wakes up, sees* **CHUCK**. *Pause.*)

TOM. Dad, / I –

JOSH. Pastor Chuck –

(**CHUCK** *gently raises his hand.* **JOSH** *and* **TOM** *fall silent.* **CHUCK** *slowly lowers his hand.*)

(*Silence.*)

(Finally:)

CHUCK. Okie doke!

> (**CHUCK** *smiles at them. He walks over to the kitchen, looking for food.*)

Big day for the two of you.

> *(Pause.)*

You know one thing I learned in my military days – the trick to jet lag is that you need to adjust your eating schedule to your destination's time zone at least twelve hours in advance. Helps so much, you wouldn't believe.

> (**CHUCK** *sees a package of ramen noodles.*)

(To **JOSH**.*)* Oh – is that yours?

> *(Pause.)*

JOSH. Yeah.

CHUCK. I just love those things, do you mind if I [have it] – …?

> *(Short pause.)*

Doctor says I shouldn't eat them, the sodium or something. But I've been good, I think. I've been good, right, Tom? Salads for lunch almost every day this month. I think I've earned it.

> (**TOM** *doesn't respond.* **CHUCK** *fills the electric kettle with water.*)

Ada told me that things got a little – tense yesterday.

> *(No response.)*

It's okay, this is a big leap you two are taking. Josh, you especially. But this is an exciting time. The time when you start to figure out who you are as an adult, what God has called you to do. The church is no longer your womb, you're becoming part of its body. You've grown so close over the years, but now – it's time to grow independently. To figure out who you both are, as men.

> (**CHUCK** *plugs in the electric kettle. He turns to* **JOSH** *and* **TOM**.*)

(During the following, he finds **TOM**'s *phone lying on the ground and picks it up, looking at it as he talks.)*

I remember the first mission I ever went on. Tom, you've heard this story so many times, you could probably tell it yourself. Tom's mom and I had driven down to Reno, we were handing out tracts to the bar crowd around midnight or so. And I had this very strict idea of how it was going to happen, we were there to hand out hundreds and hundreds of tracts, plant as many seeds as possible. So I stationed myself in front of one bar and Christine in front of another, and I pretty much just threw them at people. And at the end of the night I was so proud, I had given out something like four hundred of them, and I go to Christine and she hadn't passed out more than twenty, thirty. And I said to her – Christine, what on earth have you been doing all night?! And she told me – she had spent two hours talking to a young woman on a bench. And at the end of those two hours, they had prayed together.

(Pause.)

Your mother was such a gifted evangelist. She could witness the gospel like I've never seen. With such agility and warmth, such love, such empathy. She always hoped that we could do international missions. Would that she was still here to see it.

*(**CHUCK** hands **TOM** his phone. **TOM** looks up at him.)*

*(The electric kettle whistles. **CHUCK** goes to it, unplugging it. He pours water into the ramen noodles.)*

What is this, beef flavor? That's good. The shrimp flavor, ech. Have you had that?

(Pause.)

JOSH. Yeah.

CHUCK. It's just –. Ech.

(**CHUCK** *puts a pot holder over the ramen noodles, turns to* **JOSH**.)

CHUCK. I'm very sorry about your dad, Josh.

(*Pause.*)

JOSH. Thank you.

CHUCK. I know I've said it before, but truly – I'm sorry.

(*Pause.*)

We used to work together, did you know that?

(**JOSH** *looks at him.*)

He never told you?

(*Pause.*)

I shouldn't be surprised, I guess he just wanted to forget about me entirely.

(*Pause.*)

That grain tower complex outside of town, near the Budweiser plant, you know it? Many years ago now – twenty-five, twenty-six? – Just before I started this church, we both worked there. We had opposite shifts, I was on days and he was on nights – so we'd only see one another for a few minutes every day. But it was right around the time that I was starting to receive the gospel, and he noticed this change in me – he saw that I had this spring in my step, light in my heart. And he asked me what was going on, and I told him that I had received the good news. He was reluctant at first, but the more we talked for those few minutes every day, the more excited he got, the more he grew in the faith. And, one day, I told him that I had received my calling, that I was planning on starting a church, *this* church. An island of truth in an ocean of Mormon apostasy. And he pledged he would help me. He even offered to help me physically build this place, I swear to you. He started coming over for Bible study with Christine and I, he'd bring your mother, your infant sister. And he was sharp back then, he was...

(Thinking.)

Now what was – ... Colossians! He had the book of Colossians memorized. Every word. He was – ...

(Pause.)

I had no idea what was going on with your mother. When your father told me about her – troubles, that she had abandoned the family... I was shocked.

(Pause. **CHUCK** *goes to the noodles, lifting up the lid.)*

Little bit more.

*(***CHUCK*** *finds a place to sit.)*

It hit your dad so, *so* hard, Josh. And the next few months were – ...

(Pause.)

It was the first time I'd seen the spirit *leave* someone. When you see someone receive the gospel it's – the essence of beauty, a physical act of poetry. But when it leaves... He came to Bible study less and less, eventually fell out of contact entirely. I still count it as one of my great failures, losing him.

(Pause, looking at **JOSH**.*)*

You really didn't know any of this?

(Pause.)

JOSH. No.

(Pause.)

CHUCK. I barely recognized him when I saw him last month.

(Pause.)

JOSH. You –?

CHUCK. I saw him the day before he died, Josh.

(Pause. **CHUCK** *goes to the ramen noodles, takes the pot holder off, looks at the noodles.)*

CHUCK. That's good, there.

>   (**CHUCK** *takes the lid off, finds a fork. He sits back down with his ramen noodles, takes a bite.*)

I know there's no nutrition but I just love it. What is it about starch and salt? There's just something so hugely satisfying about it.

>   (**CHUCK** *puts down the noodles.*)

In the back of my mind – for twenty years, in the back of my mind – the memory of your father nagged at me. I felt this need to do *something*, to make him recognize that he still had this seed of faith and truth. So when you showed up here, out of the blue, when Tom first brought you here when you were – what, thirteen? – I thought, here it is, God's doing it. I thought, your dad's gotta see you, see what your faith was doing for you, how it lifted you up, how it gave you this purpose, this energy, this this this this *hope* and *optimism* – ...

>   (*Pause.*)

But when you told me how bad things had gotten – that was the moment, God was telling me to do it, to finally go to see him.

>   (**CHUCK** *eats more of the noodles.*)

That house of yours – it was farther outside of town than I remembered. How long is that drive? Forty minutes?

JOSH. Thirty.

CHUCK. Anyway I get there, and I look at him... Those vacant eyes, looking right past me. For a moment or two I wasn't sure he recognized me. I had this deep pang of guilt, knowing what you had been going through those months, years even. How could I have let you go home to this? How could I have waited this long?

>   (**CHUCK** *stands up. He looks at* **JOSH**.)

I'm so sorry, Josh.

>   (*Pause.* **JOSH** *looks up at him.*)

(After a moment, **CHUCK** *turns to* **TOM**.*)*

And suddenly I was – ... Overcome? The word sounds
indulgent but I don't know how else to describe it, I was
overcome. And I went to him and I begged him to pray
with me, I got down on the floor with him –

> (**CHUCK** *bends down to* **TOM**. **TOM** *stares at him.*
> **CHUCK** *puts his hands on* **TOM**'s *shoulders.* **TOM**
> *slowly bows his head throughout the following,*
> *burrowing his face into his knees.)*

(Closing his eyes.) And I prayed with him, I prayed: Lord
please help this man. Please forgive him, please find it
in your wisdom to pierce this man's heart, to remind
him of his goodness, to remind him of the truth he
once held so dearly in his heart, please Lord come into
his heart and make him pure again make him light
make him into your servant here on earth before it's
too late and Lord and koni ta ra fana sha ra to, ele ma
ka doni foor ta rashi ba, ta rashi ba dani ra toh ba ele
Lord Jesus korah tah ba la, korah... Korah tah ba la...

> (*Pause.* **CHUCK** *takes a breath, opening his eyes.)*

> (*He gives* **TOM** *a loving pat on the head, smiling*
> *at him, then gets up. Silence.)*

And he looked at me, and – ... Josh, I don't know
anything for certain, but I would say that he looked at
me with a pair of renewed eyes.

> (*Pause.)*

But, you know. I can't say anything for sure.

> (**CHUCK** *goes to the fridge, takes out a can of soda.*
> *He shakes it gently as he speaks.)*

It's kind of – astounding, you know? How it can all come
down to a single moment like that. The difference
between a man whose life could have ended with an
ascent to heaven, with a shedding of his earthly body
for a body of pure light... Or a life that's just – a *life,* a
series of events, just –

(**CHUCK** *opens the can of soda, putting it on the counter. He watches it as it fizzes for a moment, then stops. Pause.*)

CHUCK. *(Simply.)* Hm.

(**CHUCK** *takes one last bite of the ramen noodles, then puts it in the trash. He goes to* **JOSH**. **TOM** *hasn't moved, his face still buried in his knees.*)

Josh, I can't tell you how much I admire you for what you're doing. Tom and Ada and Denise and Marcus, they're all going to plant a seed. But you're going to be there as those seeds grow. It's what we were *meant* to do – what my Christine always wanted this church to become.

(**CHUCK** *looks at* **TOM**. *He goes to him, putting a hand on his shoulders.*)

Right, kiddo?

(**TOM** *doesn't respond.* **CHUCK** *smiles warmly at him. Pause.*)

Okie doke!

(**CHUCK** *smiles at* **JOSH**, *then grabs his soda and exits up the stairs.*)

(*A very, very long silence.* **JOSH** *and* **TOM** *don't look at one another.*)

(*Very slowly,* **TOM** *begins to lift up his head.* **JOSH** *looks at him.*)

JOSH. Tom?

(**TOM** *suddenly gets up and dashes upstairs, exiting.*)

(**JOSH** *is left alone.*)

Later That Morning.

(Packed duffel bags and backpacks are piled near the base of the stairs. ADA, DENISE, and MARCUS eat donuts as JOSH sits, anxious.)

ADA. *(To JOSH.)* Could you try calling him again, or –?

JOSH. I've been calling him all morning.

ADA. Huh. It's just like Mr. Colson is picking us up in like / fifteen –

JOSH. I don't know.

DENISE. Maybe Tom's getting a ride with someone else?

JOSH. *I don't know.* Sorry I just don't know where he is.

(Awkward pause.)

ADA. Okay well I can't wait anymore!

(ADA goes to a grocery bag near her packed duffel, brings it to them.)

You all have just been *so amazing* over these past fourteen months, I can't even tell you, so I just thought – you all deserve awards! So I made you little awards, it's stupid.

(ADA reaches into a bag, takes out a small, handmade award. JOSH looks away, lost in thought.)

The first award goes to Marcus.

MARCUS. Aw, Ada, you / didn't have to –

ADA. It's the award for "Most Improved Arabic!" Mabrook, congratulations!

(ADA hands him the award. MARCUS looks at it.)

MARCUS. Ada, this is – … I'm like – *really* touched by this.

ADA. Oh it's just stupid, I'm being stupid.

MARCUS. No, it's –. This really means something to me.

ADA. Aw.

MARCUS. I mean it.

ADA. *Aw.*

(**MARCUS** *suddenly hugs* **ADA**.)

ADA. Oh, okay.

MARCUS. *Thank you.*

ADA. Okay!

(**ADA** *pats his back,* **MARCUS** *releases her.* **ADA** *smiles at him, then pulls out another award.*)

Okay, the next award is for "Most Inspiring."

(**ADA** *smiles at* **JOSH**, *goes to him.* **JOSH** *looks at her, distracted.*)

JOSH. What?

ADA. "Most Inspiring."

JOSH. *(Taking the award.)* Oh. Thanks, this is –. Thanks.

ADA. And it's really true.

MARCUS. Totally.

ADA. You're like our mascot. Like the church mascot.

(Pause.)

JOSH. Thank you.

(**ADA** *smiles at him. She pulls out another award.*)

ADA. And now, the award for "Greenest Pants!" Mabrook!

(**ADA** *hands the award to* **DENISE**. **ADA** *and* **MARCUS** *laugh.*)

It's because of those green pants! Those pants you wear sometimes that are green!

MARCUS. That's *hilarious.*

DENISE. Oh, yeah, they're a little green. I get it.

(ADA goes back to the bag.)

ADA. There's one more, I don't know, should I take it to the airport, or –?

*(***TOM*** appears at the top of the stairs, tired and dazed, with a backpack and a duffel.* **JOSH** *doesn't see him at first.* **ADA** *sees him.*)

"Best Sense of Direction!"

(**JOSH** *looks up, sees* **TOM**. *They look at one another.*)

(**ADA** *goes to* **TOM** *with the award, pulling* **TOM** *down the stairs.*)

TOM. What?

ADA. *(Quickly.)* You get "Best Sense of Direction!" Because that time we went on the group hike and I got lost and you knew which way the car was. "Best Sense of Direction!" I made awards. Okay guys – Mr. Colson is gonna be here soon so maybe we could start taking all our stuff up / to –

MARCUS. Uh, actually – now that everyone's here?

(**MARCUS** *looks at* **ADA**.)

ADA. Oh, okay! Great!

(**MARCUS** *looks at* **DENISE**.)

MARCUS. You ready babe?

DENISE. Sure!

MARCUS. So – we have some big news to share with all of you. Some people –

(*Looking at* **ADA**.)

– already know, but…

ADA. Yep!

MARCUS. But we're really happy to tell you – Josh, Tom – that Denise – is – pregnant.

(**MARCUS** *looks at* **DENISE**, **DENISE** *smiles at him.*)

JOSH. / Oh – wow –

ADA. / Mabrook!

TOM. Congratulations.

MARCUS. Yeah! It's still early, not even three months, and we've been in touch with doctors about flying, being over there and everything, and they said it's gonna be *fine* –

ADA. *(To* JOSH *and* TOM.*)* And Marcus and Denise are actually going to be spending more time in the office, since that's just gonna be better for her and the baby.

MARCUS. It'll just be –. But yeah, we just – wanted to let you guys know!

TOM. That's – amazing –

JOSH. Congrats.

MARCUS. Thanks.

DENISE. Thanks, everyone.

ADA. *(Clapping.)* Yay!

    (Checks her watch.)

Okay guys, let's go ahead and get our luggage up there, Mr. Colson should be here in like five. Josh, is Michaela gonna see you off, or –?

    *(*TOM *looks at* JOSH. ADA *grabs her duffel, as does* MARCUS.*)*

JOSH. I, uh.

    (Pause.)

I'm not sure.

    *(*DENISE *goes for her duffel,* MARCUS *stops her.)*

MARCUS. Oh no, babe, don't lift it.

DENISE. Oh, honey, I'm really fine –

MARCUS. No! I'll get it, I'll get it! You just relax.

    *(*MARCUS *grabs both their duffels,* ADA *and* MARCUS *both exit.* JOSH *looks at* TOM, *who briefly looks at* JOSH, *then follows behind* MARCUS *and exits.)*

    *(*JOSH *grabs his duffel.)*

    *(*DENISE *looks at the award in her hands.)*

DENISE. Am I supposed to like – pack this?

JOSH. Oh, I –. I don't know, I wouldn't worry about it.

    (Pause. JOSH *looks at* DENISE.*)*

That's really great.

(DENISE *looks at him.*)

DENISE. Hm? Oh! Yeah, it's – ...

(*Pause.*)

JOSH. Your parents must be happy. What's that, the – sixth grandkid?

DENISE. Seventh. Clara has Jon, Graham, and Becky. Cindy has Zach, Anna, Rachel.

JOSH. Right, I forgot about – ... That's great.

DENISE. Yeah.

(DENISE *looks at the award in her hands.*)

I was really looking forward to this trip. Sort of felt like the last big thing I got to do before everything changes, everything...

(*Pause.*)

JOSH. Yeah, it's –

DENISE. I just think what you're doing is so cool, Josh. You're really just making something of your life, you're really *doing something.*

(*Pause.*)

Do you think my sisters are good people?

(*Pause.*)

JOSH. I – don't –

DENISE. Nevermind, I'm not sure why I said that.

(DENISE *goes to* JOSH, *putting her hands on his shoulders.*)

You're going to do *so much good*, Josh. In ten, fifteen years – I'll be here in Idaho Falls, and when I'm out driving, when I'm doing errands or driving around my kids, I'll look up toward the sky and think about you, way out there, in that village up in the mountains. I'll wonder how you're doing, what your life is like – and I'll feel so proud that I knew you once.

(*JOSH looks at her.* **DENISE** *starts to become upset. She turns away from* **JOSH**, *heading toward the bathroom.*)

JOSH. Denise –

DENISE. Just gotta pee!

(**DENISE** *exits down the hallway. After a moment,* **TOM** *enters.* **JOSH** *turns to him.* **TOM** *descends a few steps. They look at one another.*)

(*Silence.*)

(**ADA** *and* **MARCUS** *re-enter,* **TOM** *looks away from* **JOSH**, *continues down the stairs.*)

ADA. There's like string cheese, bananas, crackers maybe – check the cupboard?

(**MARCUS** *heads into the kitchenette.*)

MARCUS. Do we need like ice packs, or –?

ADA. No we can't take those.

MARCUS. Where's Denise?

JOSH. *(Pointing.)* Just in the [bathroom] –.

ADA. Someone remind me – are the tracts and Bibles upstairs or down here?

MARCUS. Upstairs, the closet behind the –

ADA. Oh right, right –

MARCUS. I'll grab 'em on our way out.

(**DENISE** *comes out of the bathroom.*)

(To **DENISE**.*)* You okay babe?

DENISE. / Yeah fine!

ADA. Okay, I think we're good then!

(*Pause. Everyone stands toward the center of the room, looking at* **ADA**.)

Now I'm not gonna make a speech or whatever. I just – …

(*Pause.*)

I know that we're just five people, five little people called to serve. But when you think about our part in the Great Commission, our place in history, how we're at the beginning of a movement that's going to change the *world*, it's…

> *(Pause, thinking.)*

And they can laugh at us all they want, but it *doesn't matter*. Because we have the *truth*. Faith in the one true message, faith in the superiority of Christian culture, and –. It's like suddenly you can see the whole planet, and your little place on it.

> *(**ADA** takes a deep breath, lost in thought. **JOSH** watches her. Pause.)*

Whoops, I made a speech! I'll shut up now. So why don't we do a quick prayer before / we –

JOSH. I think I – …

> *(Pause. **JOSH** looks at **TOM**, then at **ADA**.)*

I think I'm gonna call my sister. Let her drive me to the airport.

> *(Pause.)*

If that's okay.

> *(**TOM** and **JOSH** stare at each other. Pause.)*

ADA. Of course. That'll be nice for her.

> *(**ADA**, **DENISE**, and **MARCUS** all move away from one another, finding different places to pray.)*
>
> *(**TOM** and **JOSH** continue to stare at each other. Pause.)*

You got everything you need, right? Just text me if / you –

JOSH. I got it. Thanks.

> *(Finally, **JOSH** picks up his bag and heads toward the stairs.)*

ADA. In Jesus' name we –

> *(Suddenly **TOM** dashes to **JOSH**, wrapping his arms around him. **JOSH** wraps his arms around*

*TOM as well. They hold one another for a few
moments.)*

ADA. Oh.

(Pause.)

Oh that's so nice.

(Pause.)

It's an emotional day.

(Silence.)

(ADA, DENISE, and MARCUS all close their eyes.)

*(TOM and JOSH finally break the hug, looking at
one another, JOSH's hands still on TOM's arms.)*

Lord Jesus please come into our hearts now, fill us with
the confidence of your Spirit. Lord Jesus, we pray.

*(Finally, TOM turns away from JOSH and joins
the group. Pause.)*

*(Everyone but JOSH begins to pray. Some remain
standing, some sit, roughly in the same positions
they were in at the top of the play – all except for
JOSH.)*

(JOSH stares at TOM.)

ADA. Toru ma kala ba... Foni / sho ra...

MARCUS. Jesus pray Jesus lord God Jesus pray...

*(Slowly, JOSH picks up his duffel bag and his
backpack, still looking at TOM.)*

*(The following dialogue is continuous with no
pauses.)*

DENISE. Fo shora korla fali tah. / Kana ma shatah borah,
tene lee dinee morek ta ba. Ora tana do, falana nash
bee orandi mo. Orandi ko la tana foreshi tee, aranda
na.

TOM. Ya da eshoora, tora / ta koroosh a falo, hen ba ta ta,
la for a sha, korana talash a boreki tan lee, lee kanama
ala boh tee dan kori lo –

ADA. / Coli tarabo, coli tarabo elish ta dede ba, korna ma ba, gorta le moosh kulbi anta bolan tee do. Koosh tabi toh lash no bee. Lash no bee tori kana la –

MARCUS. Elee mamora goli yo to preni baba, elio cora tana, arash lo vana mundo malash toh ba, keena horan ah loh taba Jesus Lord borata kan non abo tori –

> (**JOSH** *finally looks away from* **TOM**, *looking upstairs. He takes out his phone.*)

ADA. / Toresh a bili fo rah, toresh ma keli ba tee, fora ele ma dora ta vatash kanini bo rana for ala faka, ele no tash woran regi fo bah ka nee, ka nee fay, ka nee lah, ka nee toranda nah bora ka la, oreshi fa! Oreshi fa no baranda fa –

TOM. / Molo fa la pola toba fo, molo po fora yelli na ma ka! Yelli allat, yelli ma bora tah leshi bino tah! Boresh a lori no, a lo bah tori dee, kan Jesus fona vendi mah, yelli allat tonana kan may boresh tan gani fay lana van –

DENISE. / Wa boratka malata, tona fah Lord God rona ma, forla vana mak. Vana mak tora. Vana mak tora fee ala kan tora, Lord God ana tan de fa tona, golana tanfee bori nana fo, anash ka be teleki can tori fish bo rana po Lord Jesus –

MARCUS. Pray Jesus pray. Ele rana for, exe fana lorex fa, korash tini falo. Korash aba tola for. Wana toh borah talaba nana ma na, mana na ma pray Jesus pray kola korash tah forandi alana no me, *alana no me pray Jesus* –

> (*Finally,* **JOSH** *slowly ascends a few steps.* **ADA**, **TOM**, **DENISE**, *and* **MARCUS** *begin to rise slightly in intensity.*)

ADA. / Goresh a bi, *goresh a bi nah.* Toli cor anana fa mi, fa mi! BLESS JESUS PRAY! HORASH A FANA TA, HORASH FA NO –

TOM. / Tora dee, tora dee for la sha bibi, *yoni nah.* Yoni nah allak! Yoni nah allak bo for a tah! FOR ALI GO RA TAH –

DENISE. / Vana mak tora! Tora lee, Jesus God, tora lee for mani voret ba! VORET BA GALEE –

MARCUS. *Tori bora, Jesus God Jesus pray! Koli foresh abi ma lora, korek tama lashti mo,* JESUS GOD ALAKA MA –

> (JOSH *is nearly at the top of the steps. He is about to make a call when suddenly:*)

ADA & MARCUS. *(In perfect unison.)* / TOREK MA, TORA KAN DO KOLI –

TOM. / BENO NO LAH, ALATI FO GONA –

DENISE. ALANA NO SAH KALASH BOH TEE –

ADA, MARCUS & DENISE. *(In perfect unison.)* / – FORESH ELE RANA –

TOM. KRANI NAH FOH LA –

> (JOSH *stops.*)

ADA, MARCUS, DENISE & TOM. *(In perfect unison.)* KANI ARANDA NA, ALISH ALANA KOR TA!

> (JOSH *turns around, looking at them.*)

(In perfect unison.) Donu la fa tomana an dee, monad alandi konesh a keli man tee. Allak yoni nah, toresh ma kelli ba! *Kanta torek ma, torek mashanta fa!*

> (ADA, MARCUS, DENISE, *and* TOM *are suddenly still, their eyes closed.*)

> (*Silence, apart from the sound of* JOSH *breathing in and out.*)

> (JOSH *drops his phone.*)

> (*Black.*)

End of Play